CHASING
A
CHINESE
DRAGON

James M Bourke

authorHOUSE®

AuthorHouse™ UK
1663 Liberty Drive
Bloomington, IN 47403 USA
www.authorhouse.co.uk
Phone: UK TFN: 0800 0148641 (Toll Free inside the UK)
*   UK Local: (02) 0369 56322 (+44 20 3695 6322 from outside the UK)*

Published by AuthorHouse 09/08/2022

ISBN: 978-1-7283-7521-2 (sc)
ISBN: 978-1-7283-7520-5 (e)

Print information available on the last page.

CONTENTS

INTRODUCTION

Chasing a Chinese Dragon is a secret agent novel. The story revolves around the quest for an elusive killer in Southeast Asia by MI6 agent Simon Grant and later by Detective Superintendent Thomas Flanagan of Scotland Yard. The suspect is seen as a dragon - not a real dragon, of course but a Chinese person with a dragon-like persona. She has embarked on a mission of retribution for the humiliation and discrimination inflicted on Chinese residents by the former British colonial rulers across Southeast Asia and by their equally corrupt successors in the present-day states of Malaysia, Singapore and Borneo. The dragon terminates several prominent British subjects visiting the region or living there as expatriates. She is fiendishly clever at locating and killing high-profile persons associated with colonial misrule. She is on a mission to pay back the old colonials and their postcolonial counterparts for years of blatant racism, shameless greed, misrule and police brutality.

The story is told by Simon Grant as he chases the elusive dragon across Southeast Asia. He frequently interrupts the story with reflections on racism, endemic corruption and misrule by the old colonial rulers of the region. He knows a good deal about the discontent of people of Chinese and Indian origin. He is unsure whether the person he is chasing is a serial killer, a subversive, or a radicalised terrorist fashioned by history.

James M Bourke
6th September, 2022.

THE SECRET WORLD OF SIS

My name is Simon Grant. I have been working in MI6 for the best part of ten years, mostly in Southeast Asia. As you are probably aware, MI6 looks after the security of British nationals and British interests overseas. Due to the Official Secrets Act, I am not free to divulge certain sensitive information concerning our mission, our modus operandi and our personnel. I do not normally talk much about my colleagues since we are, like the Freemasons, a secret organization or at least an organization with secrets. However, I have to mention one of my colleagues, my superior and mentor - Clive Bonner-Davis, Head of Oriental Operations at M16. He is a gentleman and a scholar, a graduate of Oxford University and a brilliant cricketer who once played for Middlesex.

Having completed a BA law degree course at Oxford University, I joined MI6 (now SIS) as a trainee intelligence officer. All new recruits undergo an intensive six-month training programme after which they are assigned to a particular specialisation such as computer applications, surveillance methods, intelligence gathering and analysis, counter-espionage methods and strategies, code breaking, interrogation techniques, report writing and weapons training. All trainees must have acquired at least one foreign language and they are especially interested in those who have a working knowledge of Chinese, Arabic or Russian. I was already proficient in French and German and I managed to acquire a working knowledge of colloquial Arabic before my interview.

MI6 should not be confused with MI5, which deals with threats inside the UK. MI6 operates overseas, gathering intelligence pertinent to the UK's international affairs and national interest, such as spying on Islamic terrorists in Iraq or Libya. We are intelligence officers. We collect secret intelligence and mount espionage operations overseas to detect and prevent serious crime and especially to promote and defend the national interest and economic wellbeing of the UK. We operate under a strict code of conduct set out in the Security Service Act 1989. Let me state categorically that, unlike James Bond, we do not have licence to kill. All MI6 intelligence officers are firearm-trained and are allowed to carry a weapon when on covert counter-terrorism operations. The Glock 22 is our most popular handgun. However, we hardly ever need to use it since we do not confront the enemy in open combat. Our mission is to identify and locate subversives and terrorists and it is the police or the army that do the heavy lifting. We do our homework. We know how to use spyware to track the physical and digital location of our suspects. We know how to tap into their WhatsApp, Facebook and Twitter accounts. We know the seedy hotels and 'safe houses' which terrorists frequent. Bugging such places is something we are good at. Our worst nightmare is the lone ranger who leaves no digital footprint whatever and especially the smart-ass individuals who plant fake evidence in order to lead us up the garden path.

During my probation period in London, I spent my days in that pyramidal monstrosity known as the SIS Building, overlooking the Thames at Vauxhall Cross. It is a well-known landmark in central London, headquarters of MI6. Londoners regard it with wry amusement or outright disdain and refer to it variously as Babylon-on-Thames, Gotham City or the Mayan Temple. Even visitors to London, who have no idea what MI6 is, can see that the SIS Building is a fortress, reinforced with bomb and bullet-proof walls, covered with security cameras and bristling with data protection antennae. Of course, nobody really knows what is going on inside the fortress. One sees well-dressed men in dark suits occasionally entering or leaving the building but nobody knows what they are up to, where they come from, or what their mission is. Let me explain.

MI6 works in close partnership with MI5 in Thames House on the other side of the river. Both agencies deal with threats to UK national security. Whereas MI6's primary mission is gathering intelligence overseas, MI5's mission is providing a domestic intelligence service. However, since threats to the UK such as terrorism and espionage generally originate and operate overseas, the separate role of the two agencies has begun to blur somewhat. In fact, the UK's security blanket is covered not only by MI5 and MI6 but by GCHQ and the Special Branch at Scotland Yard. I should add that Sir Alfred Naylor, who heads MI5, is a grumpy old fellow, who tries his best to dump difficult cases on us in MI6.

I know that many people think of our members as 'secret agents' like James Bond. However, our work is very different from the spy fiction one sees on television and in films. It involves tedious hours spent observing people on the move, sipping coffee in cheap cafes and reporting back to HQ on a promising development. Generally speaking, it is a hard slog with few rewarding moments to ease the tedium. Above all, successful agents have to remain invisible. Good intelligence in a vital commodity in our modern world. MI6 works secretly overseas to make the UK safer and more prosperous, developing foreign contacts, gathering intelligence, identifying risks to our national security and exploiting opportunities for trade and military cooperation. Our members are often referred to as undercover agents, spies, or snoopers, but we prefer the less loaded term 'intelligence officer'. Our mission, in most cases, is to find individuals overseas with access to secret information of value to the UK government. We also help to resolve territorial conflicts, prevent the spread of nuclear weapons, uncover hostile threats to British interests, disrupt terrorism and occasionally assist the local constabulary in tracking down criminal gangs and mischief makers. We operate under the radar and under parliamentary oversight, reflecting the values of British society within the ethical framework of a modern democracy. We take pride in the fact that MI6 is regarded as one of the best spy agencies in the world.

In the digital age the gathering of intelligence is much easier than in former times. In MI6 we have very powerful search engines, about which I am not free to discuss. We are linked to dozens of global intelligence services, such as the Joint Intelligence Organisation (JIO), the National Security Secretariat (UK), Interpol, the CIA, Mossad and the Malaysian Special Branch (SB). I can safely say to any person or body engaged in subversive activities that 'Big Brother' is watching. Even with minimal input, our analysts are very good at narrowing down the search for suspects in a particular area. By simply entering key words, the system can come up a list of possible suspects and the places they frequent. We were hoping for specific information on our suspect in Sarawak and we entered the key words: 'female, Chinese, dragon, Kuching, Prada footwear' but all we got was 'not found'. We were not really surprised since most of the data in the system comes from our agents on the ground. Of course, our data bases are constantly being hacked by hostile states such as Russia, China and Iran.

In London, we also work in partnership with the Metropolitan Police. Each week, my boss Bonner-Davies meets with his counterpart in Scotland Yard, Detective Superintendent Thomas Flanagan. They are not only colleagues but close friends. Flanagan was born and raised in London but his parents came to London from Dublin during the building boom following World War 2. As a young man, he joined the Metropolitan Police and, in his years on the beat, he got to know London like the back of his hand. Not surprisingly, he became a senior officer in the Homicide and Serious Crime Command at the Met i.e., police headquarters in Victoria Street.

I know that Flanagan thinks it odd that MI6 should have such a very public face as the SIS Building. For him, the oddest thing about the SIS Building is not its massive architecture but the sheer incompetence of its upper echelon, mostly Old Etonians and Old Harrovians, who speak Public School English and wear pin-striped suits made by bespoke tailors in Jermyn Street. He prefers to speak plain English with traces of an Irish accent. He is great fun and tells us all that 'any fool can be serious.' I have spent many a joyous session with him in Waxy O'Connor's Pub in Soho.

I am sometimes asked why I decided to join MI6. I must confess that I did so not out of patriotic fervour to protect the British people and British interests. Rather I think it had more to do with my fondness for reading crime fiction. From about the age of fourteen I developed an inordinate interest in stories about gangsters, cold-blooded killers, famous detectives and spies. I had read many vintage spy novels such as Joseph Conrad's 'The Secret Agent' (1907), Sex Rohmer's villainous tale 'The Mystery of Dr. Fu-Manchu' (1916) and several volumes of Sir Arthur Conan Doyle's stories. Moreover, I had a burning desire to travel abroad and experience the joy of visiting exotic places. I wanted to walk in the footsteps of the great travel writers, in particular those who ventured across the Near East, British India and Southeast Asia. For reasons that I cannot explain, key words like the 'Ottoman Empire, the Raj, the Straits Settlements, the White Rajahs, Makassar, Sarawak and Sabah' fascinated me as I read with great eagerness the memoirs and writings of Alfred R. Wallace, Joseph Conrad, Alexander Kinglake, Lawrence of Arabia, Rudyard Kipling, W. Somerset Maugham, Wilfrid Thesiger and Eric Newby. Of course, everyone at MI6 had read Graham Greene's spy classics 'The Confidential Agent' (1939) and 'The Third Man' (1950). My favourite author was and still is Sir Arthur Conan Doyle. I have read all his stories about the world's most famous detective, Sherlock Holmes. However, I did not want to be a detective; I wanted to be a secret agent, even though my parents hated the idea. However, looking back now, having spent ten years in MI6, I have no regrets. I think perhaps my English teacher at Ampleforth College got it right when he said: 'We are what we read.'

Moreover, living in London had become rather tiresome. It is a wonderful city but living there is not a cascade of rainbows. In the eighteenth century, Dr. Johnson said: 'When a man is tired of London, he is tired of life.' Well, we are no longer living in the 18th century and I expect a lot of Londoners today are tired of hearing Dr. Johnson's bland assertion. I know I am. I could never see myself facing the daily grind of travelling to work on British Rail, embracing the London rat race, putting up with the horrid pollution, experiencing the sheer awfulness of living in city bursting at the seams and observing the dejection etched on the faces of its inhabitants. It was all too much for me. I wanted out. The absence of light was killing me. I was tired of London but contrary to Dr. Johnson, I was not tired of life. I needed variety, colour, clear skies and smiling faces. I needed to go somewhere different, beyond the grey horizon.

I suppose at a subconscious level I probably felt a moral imperative to do something useful in my life. At that time many countries were facing grave problems due to famine, disease, terrorism, climate change, crime, racism and endemic corruption. One cannot sit on the fence forever. Evil has to be confronted in places riven by terrorism, civil strife and the suppression of 'freedom'. I felt that I should heed the wise words of Edmund Burke: 'The only thing necessary for the triumph of evil is for good men to do nothing.' I probably saw myself as a cog in the great wheel of humanitarianism, human rights and a just society. To me, MI6 is a mechanism for doing good. It uncovers and disables terrorists who aim to disrupt the social fabric through violence. We all need protection from the mad idealists who maim and murder innocent people, terrorise communities and turn a normal state into a living hell. Serving in MI6 is a vocation just like our medical services, social welfare, nursing, teaching, etc. all of which require exceptional dedication. We work on the front line, keeping a close watch on the enemy, doing our best to gather vital intelligence on many fronts but at all times remaining below the radar.

With a song in my heart, I was happy to go where many of my forebears had gone before – to what was once the great British Empire on which the sun never set. I would gladly go to fight the foreign foe, preferably anywhere east of Suez but, of course, I had no choice in the matter.

TO SARAWAK

In 1998 I was posted to Sarawak, a land of spectacular natural scenery on the island of Borneo. It took me some time to adjust to the heat and humidity and a way of life that was both strange and enchanting. For the first few years there, I had a relatively quiet and uneventful time but in 2002 all of that suddenly changed when I was requested to assist in a manhunt for a serial killer. MI6 does not normally get involved in crime detection and prevention overseas. However, we are sometimes requested by the local police department to help in tracking down serial killers, drugs barons, bank robbers, rapists and especially those with links to the Mafia or subversive organizations. Needless to say, we are constantly being watched by secret agents from other countries, in particular the US, Russia and China. Espionage is a risky business. I am not free to disclose how many of our agents have been captured, charged with spying and imprisoned.

In case your geography is somewhat rusty, I shall at various points in the narrative include some background information. Borneo is a very large island, three-times bigger than the UK, on the equator, to the east of Singapore. North Borneo consists of the East Malaysian states of Sarawak and Sabah, with tiny Brunei wedged in between them. The rest of the island belongs to Indonesia. Most of Borneo is covered in the oldest and most spectacular rainforest in the world. It is home to 200 ethnic groups, the main ones being the Malay, Chinese, and indigenous people. The island was divided between the British and the Dutch in 1896, when land grabbing was popular. Sarawak was ceded to the English adventurer, James Brooke (the White Rajah) by the Sultan of Brunei, while Sabah was leased to the North Borneo Chartered Company by the Sultan of Sulu. Later, Sarawak and Sabah became British Crown colonies, under a British government official called a Resident. The Malay states were semi-independent, each with its Sultan as head of state but the real power rested in the hands of the Resident. Brunei was a British 'protectorate' – a nice term for a state which is controlled and protected by another. In 1963, both Sabah and Sarawak opted to join the Federation of Malaysia, which many permanent residents at that time deemed a bad move. It seems they were told it was a 'temporary arrangement.' However, we know very well that there is nothing more permanent than a 'temporary arrangement'. I shall not list all the complaints I have heard about misrule by the Federal government since our role in MI6 is to maintain friendly relations with Malaysia. However, one cannot ignore the rape of the rainforest in Sarawak. Sadly, much of Borneo's rainforest is being depleted by logging, resulting in a massive loss of habitat for its forest dwellers, the Orang Ulu, and for its unique wildlife – the orangutans, monitor lizards, horned frogs, numerous reptiles and its splendid butterflies and hornbills.

I should add that MI6 looks after the wellbeing of all British subjects living and working not only in North Borneo but across Southeast Asia. During the colonial period, the British officers and officials would complain of the hardship of living and working 'under the alien sky' while forgetting that they were the aliens. As in British India, they were very good at looking down on the 'lazy natives' and displaying a 'paternalistic duty' towards the coloured races in Borneo, the Malay states, Brunei and Singapore. Today, all those states enjoy independence but for economic reasons the Foreign Office and MI6 will always take the side of the establishment. It is no longer a case of racial supremacy; it is a matter of pragmatism and realpolitik; we always try to be helpful and uncritical of misrule in our former colonies especially those with great natural resources.

I was based in Kuching, the capital of Sarawak but I had a roving commission to assist with intelligence gathering across the parts of Southeast Asia that were once Crown colonies or British protectorates. They include Singapore, the Malay States and the North Borneo states of Sarawak, Sabah and independent Sultanate of Brunei. MI6 has agents gathering intelligence in each of those territories. They all work under the radar in various locations about which I cannot comment.

I shall not say much about my family background since it is a long story. It will suffice to say that my father is a proud Irishman who came to the UK as a teenager from Mallow in County Cork. My mother is a proud French woman who came originally from Saint-Malo in Brittany. My sister Grace and I are London Irish of a somewhat confused identity being partly Irish, French and British. Like Thomas Flanagan, I can claim to be Irish or Anglo-Irish, more Anglo than Irish. My family belonged to the Ascendency in Ireland, which Brendan Behan refers to as 'Protestants on horses.' In 1922, my grandparents decided it was time to leave County Cork as many of the 'big houses' belonging to the landed gentry were being set on fire by the IRA. They settled in Shropshire, where my father got involved in horse training and racing and where my sister and I grew up, immersed in country pursuits – horse riding, angling, shooting and hill climbing. My father was an agnostic Anglican and my mother a devout Roman Catholic. I was educated at Ampleforth College where I excelled at rugby and cricket but did less well at book learning. The problem was that I spent a lot of my study time reading curious books instead of swatting up for my O-level and A-level exams. I still have some of the progress reports which my old form master, Mr. Gunton, sent to my parents. One says: 'I regret to inform you that Simon is a lazy fellow, much given to day dreaming and idle chatter. He needs pushing.' I certainly got my fair share of pushing at Ampleforth, both on the rugby pitch and in the classroom. It was all done in the name of character formation, just like every other public school in England. However, I have to say that the tuition was exceptionally good as was the food.

Eventually, in my final year I applied myself diligently to my studies and achieved A grades in English, French and History which got me into Oxford University much to the surprise of my form master and ever much more to the astonishment and joy of my parents.

At Oxford, I read law in Magdalen College over four years, including a year abroad at the Sorbonne Law School. At that time Oxford was known as a 'seat of learning' where the goal of education across all disciplines was first and foremost the cultivation of wisdom. The Magdalen Law School is simply amazing. It is staffed by world-leading academics whose names appear on many law books. The syllabus has a broad span. There, in that hothouse of great legal minds, you learn as much about philosophy, sociology and politics as you do about law. At undergraduate level the main focus is on common law but other electives may be taken. As I was especially interested in criminal law, I took that elective in my third year. All coursework is assessed by regular assignments and a final examination leading to the degree BA Jurisprudence.

My graduation paper on 'The Criminal Mind' caused quite a stir in that it challenged the prevailing viewpoint that psychopaths are 'born not made'. My thesis was that serial killers were victims of their history. I rejected the assumption that crime, emotional distress and abnormal behavior were due to an innate disorder in the brain. In order to tap into the mind of the killer and uncover the psychological factors that shaped their persona, I interviewed a large sample of serial killers serving a life sentence in British prisons, including the infamous 'moors murderer' Ian Brady. I discovered that all of his subjects were, in their formative years, victims of historical abuse – political and cultural abuse by the establishment. The psychopaths in my study had been emotionally disturbed, conditioned and radicalised by their nation's history. Put simply, my finding was that if you kick a dog often enough, one day it will bite you. We are all, to some extent, victims of our history and it is 'bad history' that can push an individual into being a very dangerous person. All the subjects in my study claimed that they had been dealt a bad hand in life. They were tormented by legacy issues. In the past, their ancestors had been persecuted, their land had been confiscated and they had been forced to leave their homeland. For them, the past was never past. It lived in the unconscious mind and anyone perceived to be associated with past misrule, exploitation, or discrimination should be called out, punished and even exterminated. The victims of misrule tend to become alienated and believe in the Law of Talon, which in modern idiom translates as 'an eye for an eye'. They do not see themselves as killers but as executioners. My study found that the subjects I interviewed showed no remorse for their action. They said that it was their duty to seek retribution for the wrongs inflicted on their race. It was a moral imperative.

My study was highly praised by my tutor, Dr. Bell, who decided to have it published in *The British Journal of Criminology*. It was not very well received by readers of that illustrious journal. They held that psychopathic behaviour was due to a genetic disorder in the left hemisphere of the brain. They scoffed at the idea of a serial killer being conditioned by history. For them, psychopaths were born not made. They had ample proof that all serious crime resulted from innate predestined grooves in the brain. They quoted the famous line attributed to Ian Brady, who, pointing to his head said: 'It all takes place up here.'

There was much rejoicing in my family when I graduated and could henceforth add the letters 'BA Oxon' after my name. That academic badge gave me enormous pride as did the testamur displayed on the wall in my study. It was the badge of academic distinction which opened the door to top positions in criminal law or psychiatry. However, a career in clinical or criminal psychiatry had little appeal for me. I am an adventurous soul and I wanted the opportunity to see the world. In particular, I was attracted to Southeast Asia, due largely to the superb wildlife documentary *Zoo Quest for a Dragon*, produced by David Attenborough for the BBC. That documentary was magic. I too, wanted to travel into the heart of Borneo to see for myself the exotic wild life and the flora and fauna of the rainforest. As a teenager, I had read the early colonial history of the region and in particular the story of James Brooke, the White Rajah of Sarawak and the dubious deeds of the North Borneo Chartered Company in Sabah. I had read the personal accounts of the early explorers who left vivid personal accounts of Borneo's native rainforest people - the Orang Ulu – as well as a record of jungle exploration, natural history, missionary activity, early settlements, the spice trade and much else in that enchanting land. I had read Conrad's great oriental novels *An Outcast of the Islands* and *Almayer's Folly*. Beyond Borneo, I was fascinated by the early history and topography of the majestic Malay States, the model city of Singapore and the magical islands of Indonesia where the great naturalist A.R. Wallace spent years working on his theory of evolution.

No words can describe the sheer beauty and diversity of Borneo. It has magnificent rainforest teeming with life and native tribes living contentedly off the fruits of the rainforest. The indigenous people are poor and uneducated by our standards but they seem happy and welcoming. Some of them attended Mission Schools and having acquired a knowledge of English moved to the towns where they work on building sites and in other manual jobs. It was not long before I noticed that there was an undercurrent of disharmony among the various races there – the Malays, the Chinese, the Indians and the indigenous people. For instance, every taxi driver would tell you that Malaysia is a very corrupt country. The Chinese and the Indians complained of gross discrimination; they said that they were second-class citizens, ruled by a xenophobic 'ship of fools' in Putrajaya. The indigenous people in both parts of Malaysia were regarded as a lower form of life, only slightly above the great apes. There was discontent in Paradise over endemic racism, corruption and even gross violations of basic human rights. But, of course, in MI6 we tend to ignore such anti-government rhetoric as the voice of leftist malcontents bent on undermining the legitimate government in Malaysia, Brunei and even Singapore. MI6 has a duty to maintain good relations with all of our former colonies in Southeast Asia. After all, surely good economic and trading ties between us and them are paramount. In a turbulent world, one cannot yield to the voice of dissent. What we do in MI6 comes under the rubric of diplomacy. We do nor ruffle feathers or berate our allies, even when thy step over the line of common decency. I suppose we all pursue wisdom in our own different ways. We all seek to come to terms with the dilemmas in our lives, seeking inner peace and wisdom in a world that offers neither. Many so-called democracies are ruled by corrupt political parties and little pharaohs. As a result, some members of society will rise up in anger, become alienated and as a result, lose all moral compass. The angry ones - the dispossessed, the abused, the marginalised, and the victims of postcolonial misrule become radicalised over a variety of perceived wrongs. It may be over racial issues, religious issues, social issues or very often legacy issues arising from colonial ideology – the superior race looking down on those of a different ethnic and cultural heritage, in a word, the apartheid mindset in all but name. In Malaysia, some people of Chinese origin, Indian origin, Indonesian origin, as well as the indigenous people tend to see themselves as victims of an uncaring establishment and they may resort to subversive activities in order to seek retribution for discrimination, abuse, exploitation and misrule. Of course, they are a minority and we call them criminals, subversives, terrorists, jihadists and other names and they in turn call us neo-Nazis, white scum, Imperialist pigs, fascists, war-dogs and supremacist bigots. And so, we live in turbulent times, with radicalised people becoming ever more assertive, more desperate and more rebellious. Hence, the need for a body such as MI6 to protect the ship of state, its crew and the common people. The story which I am about to share with you is a good example of alienation, disaffection and retribution. It is about a Chinese rebel who seems to possess all the instinctive cunning of a dragon.

Sometimes it is hard to say which side is the more criminal, our side or theirs. Our democracy has become wafer thin and sometimes in MI6 we are expected to defend the indefensible. In my humble opinion, Britain today is a very sick nation but of course, I should not say that. However, I should like to make it clear that in MI6, we are not xenophobic bigots or right-wing extremists. Our mission is to maintain the statues quo and prevent mayhem and loss of life. We work with and behalf of the overseas government, the army and the police. Our mission is to track down and neutralise those individuals or groups that use violence and intimidation in the pursuit of political aims. I should stress that we do not engage in the national political battles that are a feature of our former colonies.

Working in intelligence gathering is no ordinary job. It calls for great dedication and exceptional problem-solving competence. It is also a high-risk occupation. On joining M16, I was asked if I had a 'heart of steel'. At the time I thought that was an odd question but now I know that every secret agent needs a heart of steel in order to survive. Certainly, MI6 is not for weaklings nor people seeking movie star fame. Unlike James Bond, we do not chase criminals in a classy amphibious Lotus car across rooftops and rivers. MI6 agents do not seek the limelight; they operate unseen. During my time in Malaysia, everyone assumed that I was an educational consultant with the British Council. That was my cover but in fact I had no links whatever to the British Council.

I mention all of the above so that you may better understand the context to my story, details of which I shall attempt to share with you in following pages. It is basically the account of a mission to which I was assigned while I was a MI6 agent in Malaysia - an episode in which MI6 and Scotland Yard played a major role, while MI5 under Sir Albert Naylor, played a minor role. My boss, Bonner-Davis and I were at the centre of the storm. We were chasing an unknown killer who was as cunning as a dragon. We had no idea who he or she was nor what was motivating them. All we knew was that the suspect was driven by some extreme cause or ideology and was well versed in political assassinations. And make no mistake, it was a real storm which sent shock waves across Southeast Asia. It also caused much criticism of M16 in general and me in particular. In the British press, I was accused of professional incompetence in letting the dragon through the net.

3
A HIDDEN HAND STRIKES

It was mid-summer and the heat in London was infernal. The SIS Building has every conceivable amenity except air-conditioning. Even with widows wide open there was hardly a flicker of a breeze. The heat and humidity were overbearing. The cleaning staff complained of the heat. Our secretary, Miss Denby sighed: 'It's like a pizza oven in here.' However, my colleagues bore the heat with fortitude. After all, it was mild compared to the torrid heat of the Malay States, Borneo and Indonesia. Neckties were worn loosely while overhead ceiling fans whirred and purred. Beyond the great pile of the SIS Building something really important was taking place – the test match at Lords.

'Blimey, the Aussie wankers have taken another wicket,' moaned 'Smokey' Smithers, my project manager.

'Language, old boy! Let's maintain some sobriety in here at least,' I responded in jest. I was not in the least perturbed about our dismal performance in the test match nor the stifling weather. I love the game of cricket but I had more urgent matters to attend to than moaning about our inept performance in the test match. At that time, MI6 had a dozen men on data-gathering missions all over Southeast Asia keeping a close eye on political, economic, military and educational developments in the region. That is what we do. But we had just received news of a serious security situation in far-away Borneo. We were informed that a prominent British businessman, Sir Basil Green, suddenly went missing in Sarawak. The local police were at sixes and sevens, not knowing what to report to the High Commission in Kuala Lumpur. The man had simply disappeared without a trace. Sir Basil was 'an old colonial' whose family had established a large sago plantation near Sibu during the Rajah Brooke era. He also owned several sago processing plants in the area. He was a very wealthy man but he was not known for his generosity to the Melanau workers in the sago fields and factories. He no longer lived in Sibu but was a frequent visitor to the town. He lived in London where he was something of a toff. He had a fine Edwardian townhouse in fashionable West Hampstead. He was a man of the world, living in style on inherited wealth. He dined out most evenings and he had a fondness for Italian cuisine, French cognac, Cuban cigars and leggy oriental women. He was well looked after by his long-serving housekeeper, Mrs. Bates.

In Sarawak, the local police combed the whole Sibu area looking for Sir Basil but without success. They were convinced that sooner or later they would find a badly beaten corpse in the muddy waters of the Rajang River. It might never be found since it would almost certainly have been already devoured by a crocodile. However, neither the Melanau fishermen nor the sago workers had seen anything abnormal on the river or in the mangrove swamps. While in London, I was asked to look into the matter. I very quickly discovered that Sir Basil was alive and well. The local police chief in Sibu, Inspector Abu Bakar, had obviously overlooked the obvious, namely that the missing person had simply made a speedy exit back to London. That simple fact was immediately confirmed when I checked the passenger manifest of all flights out of Kuching the previous day. Sir Basil's name was listed on an AirAsia flight to Kuala Lumpur and on a Malaysian Airlines flight to London. Clearly, he had left Kuching in great haste and must have had a good reason to do so. He was a wanted man. Inspector Abu Bakar seemed relieved that the fugitive was on his way to the UK and no longer in his jurisdiction. He said to me: 'Sir Basil is now in your court. I expect MI6 will uncover the reason for his hasty departure. I suspect that the Chinese mafia have something to do with it. In Sarawak, we have to live with the 'yellow peril'. But of course, one should say such things in public.'

'One should not say such things in private,' I snapped in response. I knew only too well the deep-seated racism that existed not only in East Malaysia but across the whole Federation. The one thing I can say about MI6 is that it is not racist. In that respect, it is quite different from the old colonial administration that once ruled over much of Southeast Asia. It also differs from the ruling coalition called the 'Barisan National' (National Front) which has ruled Malaysia since 1973 and which adopts and still implements the same race-based policies as its predecessor, 'The Alliance Party' and before that, the British colonial regime. Several critics of modern Malaysia claim that British misrule was replaced by far more insidious Malay misrule. Of course, on such matters, we in MI6 do not comment. I regard such sweeping generalizations as highly dubious.

I was shocked to discover that Sir Basil Green had arrived back in London in great haste. It appears that he was fleeing before an unseen assassin. Naturally, I shared my concern for his safety with my boss in London who in turn alerted Flanagan in Scotland Yard and Det. Inspector Naylor in MI5. I was so concerned that I decided to remain in London a week or two longer than planned. My boss, Bonner-Davies, was quite shocked when I suddenly appeared at SIS. He assumed that I had taken annual leave and was on my way to Shropshire for a spot of fly fishing.

'Sorry old boy for not keeping you in the loop,' I said. 'We must talk. I am not on leave. I am on duty. Can you put me up here for a few days while I check on Sir Basil? It seems that in his case, time is of the essence. I mean, his time on this planet may be running out.'

I had barely spoken those words when the telephone rang. It was Flanagan. There was no greeting or chit chat. 'Get your boots on old boy,' he said to Bonner-Davies. 'There's been a serious incident at 49 Broadhurst Gardens, West Hampstead. A gentleman by the name of Sir Basil Green.'

Bonner-Davies and I lost no time in reaching Sir Basil's residence. We leapt out of the car, dashed up the steps and pounded on the front door which was instantly opened by Mrs. Bates.

'Something awful has happened to Sir Basil,' she muttered pointing in the direction of the upper rooms. Her face had blanched and her eyes were set in a stare of horror. 'He seems to be having a heart attack or something. You may be too late. The medics should be here any minute.' We bounded up the staircase and burst into the bedroom. We found Sir Basil lying prone on the bed, fully clothed. He was clearly at death's door. His face was pallid and contorted like an El Greco painting. His eyes were glazed and clouded.

'Sir Basil, old boy! What's happened?' Bonner-Davies pleaded. There was no response. He repeated the question and in a barely audible voice Sir Basil whispered the words 'damned dragon'. Those were the only and last words spoken by him. A moment later, he was dead. Det. Inspector Naylor from MI5 and his Rapid Response team had already arrived. The coroner, Dr. Eltham also arrived shortly after that. He was a man of few words. He hovered over the dead body and said instantly 'It's an acid job. Somebody has smeared a fast-acting agent on his face. It causes instant blindness followed by convulsions, loss of consciousness, paralysis and death due to respiratory failure. Of course, we shall have to conduct a forensic post-mortem,' he said with the air of man weary of making such sad pronouncements. The body was removed in a black bag and Naylor's men had already begun collecting items for forensic examination. Not surprisingly, Dr. Eltham was right. The post-mortem results from Sir Basil's body showed that he had died within 20 minutes of the attack. An unknown person had obviously come at Sir Basil from behind and sprayed or wiped his face with an acid identified as the deadly VX nerve agent. Clearly, Sir Basil had not died of natural causes. Clearly, he had been killed by an unknown hand. However, we wondered what to make of his dying words, 'damned dragon'. Perhaps he was hallucinating. On that score Det. Inspector Naylor said sardonically: 'We do not have the time, resources or inclination to go chasing a dragon. In any event, this is a job for Scotland Yard on instructions from MI6.'

Mrs. Bates was most distressed. She had no idea that Sir Basil's life was in danger. That afternoon, she had been tending roses in the rear garden. At 4 p.m. she returned to the kitchen where she intended to bake a cake. Suddenly, she heard a great commotion upstairs including loud banging on a door. She immediately climbed the stairs and knocked on Sir Basil's bedroom door. There was no response. She then gently opened the door and peered inside. The room seemed empty but there was the sound of water splashing in the adjoining bathroom. She found Sir Basil, fully clothed, bent over the wash-hand basin, furiously splashing water over his face. He was groaning in agony, like a wounded animal. His cries were pitiful.

'My God! Whatever's happened sir?' she asked. 'You seem in a state.'

'Someone grabbed me from behind and smeared my face with acid or something toxic. I can't see a thing and I'm feeling queasy. Go down and call 999 at once.'

Mrs. Bates did as she was bid. The police and an ambulance arrived within minutes. Before leaving the house, we tried our best to console her. She seemed to think that she was somehow negligent. She had been tending her roses when she should have been looking after her master's welfare. She had not seen nor heard anyone enter or leave the house. It was all most peculiar - a dastardly deed by an unseen hand. Moreover, nobody in the street had seen anything suspicious. The assailant had vanished without a trace. It looked like the perfect murder. No blood on the carpet. No stains on the bed or clothing. No fingerprints anywhere. No weapon. However, with his instinct for noticing things that others overlooked, Flanagan pointed out a possibly significant item. With his eagle eye, he found fresh female footprints on the landing which, in spite of Mrs. Bates' cleaning, was covered in a thin layer of dust. They clearly belonged to a small female foot and might well reveal something about the suspect. The shoe impressions were included in the items sent to our forensic laboratory.

I was baffled by Sir Basil's reported last words, 'dammed dragon'. To me they denoted a Chinese person, rather than a real dragon. I knew that in Chinese culture and astrology, the dragon plays an important role. Perhaps, at some stage, those words might point us in the direction of the suspect.

On our way back to headquarters, Bonner-Davies, Flanagan and I stopped off at Brown's Hotel in Mayfair for 'high tea' – an English invention as sacred as cricket. Det. Inspector Naylor never joins us on such frivolous occasions. He is, I understand, a strict Presbyterian of the old school in Bristol, who regards a visit to a public house or a hotel bar an abomination. Alas, neither Flanagan nor I have any such scruples. Those of us in the security game are treated as honoured guests at several London hotels and restaurants. We always got a warm welcome from Antonio, the head waiter at Brown's. We would be given a complimentary malt whisky and a generous discount on food. Antonio was indebted to Flanagan, who had at some time in the past got him off a charge of supplying cannabis to his wealthy patrons. In our line of business, one has to give a little to get a little. You have to keep your ear to the ground. Our best informers are waiters, barmen, taxi drivers and barbers. As we were leaving, Flanagan said to Antonio 'If you happen to see a dragon, do let us know.'

He replied 'Si, Senor Thomas. Of course!'

Antonio had no idea what Flanagan meant but he knew that the English often spoke in riddles. For instance, in England it rains 'cats and dogs' whereas in Italy it rains 'pots and pans'. Surely the Italian idiom was much more meaningful. At least Flanagan spoke the Queen's English clearly unlike many toffs in MI6 who hardly moved their lips in order to maintain the 'stiff upper lip' of the well-bred English gentleman.

A few days later I returned to Kuching and I contacted Bonner-Davies right away to remind him to check out the source of our suspect's shoes - a possibly vital clue to her identification. Forensics found that the foot impressions found on the landing in Sir Basil's house were those of a female foot, size 6 and furthermore that such shoes were unique to Prada. Footprints can be almost as revelatory as finger prints. I discovered that only one shop in Kuching sold Prada shoes. I contacted the owner who told me that in the past not many people in the city bought Prada shoes but in recent times many merchants had become millionaires due to the boom resulting from the sale of timber and palm oil. They suddenly acquired a taste for luxury goods, such as Rolex and Patek Philippe watches and the top-of-the-line brands in clothing and footwear. When I showed him the footwear impression in question, he smiled and said: 'Oh yes! Those are Prada all right, in fact, a limited edition costing $1,500; popular with our wealthy Datuks, Bruneian upper crust and Russian tourists.' Sadly, he had no sales record. All his clients paid in cash but he vaguely remembered a certain tall young Chinese lady buying a pair some months previously. She spoke Hokkien and she said she was in a rush to catch a flight back to Sibu. Later that day I called Bonner-Davies and said: 'The person we are looking for may be a young Chinese lady. She has great taste; she wears Prada.'

'I thought you said she was a dragon. Do dragons wear Prada?' he quipped.

It was not much of a clue, really. There were probably a thousand young Chinese ladies in Kuching belonging to wealthy merchant families that could well afford a pair of Prada shoes. Still, in our line of business every little helps. However, it seemed reasonable to assume that no criminally-minded young lady would ever wear the same shoes again if she decided to embark on another killing mission. What really shocked me was the fact that the suspect, the so-called dragon, was possibly living in Kuching where I was stationed. Did she know of my existence I wondered and if so, could I possibly be her next target? Strange things happen in Sarawak. People sometimes disappear and it is assumed that they have been abducted by the 'hantu' (i.e., evil spirits) who dwell in the rainforest. In MI6, however, we know that the evil spirits are criminal elements, such as the local Mafia, or political subversives or serial killers.

ETHNIC CLEANSING

Sarawak is famous for its vast pristine rainforest – a magical world, stunning in its beauty and rich in the variety of its plant and animal life. Its ancient trees are truly awesome and its hardwoods were gold dust in the eyes of the 'Alliance Party' which ruled Sarawak from 1952 to 1973. It was said that its members were very corrupt and used vote-buying tactics in order to win elections. The same was said of its successor, the 'Barisan National' (National Front) whose members became a class of millionaires from 1987 onwards by selling logging concessions which raised almost $20 billion each year. By 2000, over three million acres of forest had been acquired by the government. Of course, every dog in the street knew that the members of the 'golden circle' in the State Assembly were nothing more than thieves and that their great scheme for rural development was nothing more than an illegal land grab. The dense forest of the interior had, since colonial times, been designated as the 'customary land' of the indigenous people, in particular the nomadic Penan, Iban and the inland Dayak tribes. They had lived off the fruits of the forest for centuries and their ownership of the forest had never been disputed by the White Rajahs. Their abode was the forest and, in their culture, it was a holy place, lush, pure and sacred, home to their ancestors and many 'hantu' (spirits). Their harmonious way of life had never changed until the bulldozers moved in. The ruling elite chose to overlook that fact and thus began the rape of the rainforest. The logging companies began clearing the ancient trees which were floated on barges down the Baram River to Miri for export to Japan and Europe. Naturally, the Penan people protested vigorously and began blockading all entry points and dirt roads leading to their ancestral land. A long confrontation between them and the State of Sarawak ensued. That 'confrontasi' over logging was blamed on Bruno Manser, the Swiss activist for rainforest preservation. He had lived among the Penan tribes in the Baram and Limbang areas, fomenting anti-logging protest and organising blockades against the 'invaders', especially the Miri-based Interhill Group. The elusive Manser was declared persona non grata by the State Governor; in fact, he was regarded as 'the most wanted man in Malaysia.' It was also put about that the protest was funded and supported by the wealthy Chinese in Marudi, who regarded deforestation as an environmental disaster.

The standoff over logging was still in full spate when a certain Mr. Colin Reynolds arrived on the scene. He was the PR manager of a real estate company in London, Relco International, which specialised in the acquisition of property and land; in other words, its business was vulture fund management. Reynolds was an ostentatious man of the world, often seen in the cocktail bar of the Ritz, talking politics and venting his rage on the EU for the sad state of the British economy. He stood out even in the street, by his conservative attire - a Burberry trench coat, a bowler hat and always sporting a silver-mounted cane. Reynolds had served as an officer in the Royal Marines but was dismissed because of an offensive article he had published in 'The Daily Dispatch'. His article, entitled 'Taking back the Empire', claimed that the Third World began at Calais. His concluding remarks sum up the tenor of the piece: 'Clearly, our former colonies in Africa, the Middle East and Southeast Asia are rogue nations, corrupt to the core. Of course, ruling the races of those ungodly lands is like dancing on the head of a nest of snakes. In the interest of restoring democracy, we may have to send in the gun boats once more.' To their credit, the British Army generals dismissed Reynolds for such rampant racism and xenophobia. However,

Reynolds believed in the maxim that you cannot keep a good man down. He joined the Tory party and became press secretary to two PMs. He still wrote the odd political essay for 'The Daily Dispatch'. He had, over the years, written disparagingly about the 'Yellow Peril', castigating not only the rulers of Red China but also the Chinese diaspora in Singapore, Malaysia, Borneo and Indonesia. He should have been charged for inciting racial and religious hatred, but at that time, Sinophobia, Islamophobia, and anti-Semitism were all the rage in Britain. He referred to the Chinese as an 'alien race' who had no right of abode in Britain. They did not belong in the white 'national community' of British people.

It seems that Relco was unaware of Reynolds' neo-Nazi views. In 2003, he was sent to Malaysia in order to help the government decide on how best to explore and exploit the rainforest in Sarawak and Sabah. His mission was to estimate the extent and the potential valuation of the forest that could be earmarked for 'selective logging' with a view to clearing as much of it as possible for palm-oil plant cultivation. Before proceeding to Kuching, he had been briefed by both the Forestry Department and the Finance Department of the Federal government in Putrajaya. He was advised to take the greatest caution in Sarawak as there had been trouble with the Penan natives in the Baram District over logging. They had mounted a blockade of several dirt tracks into the rainforest.

Reynolds had several meetings with the State Governor and the Forestry Department in Kuching. He was told that the objective was to boost the economy by having parts of the forest cleared and the land converted to palm oil production. Everyone would benefit, especially the Penan and the Orang Ulu (Dayaks). There would be billions of dollars for rural development, for infrastructure and for schools and hospitals. At that time, almost 10 percent of the rainforest had been uprooted and Reynolds estimated that at least $20 billion annually could be raised from the sale of timber and palm oil. It was music to the ears of the ruling elite not only in Kuching but in Putrajaya. They would each get a slice of the salami.

Reynolds made his way to Miri and from there he travelled by speedboat to Marudi, where the District Officer had arranged for him to meet the Penan tribal leaders whom he hoped to persuade to end their protest by spelling out the great benefits that would accrue to them from the billions of dollars which would result from 'selective logging' and the much-needed employment on the palm oil plantations which would follow. All they had to do was to call off their illegal blockade and allow the logging companies access to the forest. He would tell them that before very long they would be as wealthy as their neighbours across the border in oil-rich Brunei. Reynolds was about to negotiate a win-win agreement and in order to reinforce his message, he had not come empty handed. Gifts of cigarettes, Lipton tea, alcohol and beads would be presented to the tribal chiefs. A little bit of bribery always goes a long way in Borneo.

As the speedboat approached the jetty in Marudi, a large gathering of semi-naked Penan people gazed curiously at the approaching speedboat which was accompanied by a police escort. They wondered who the stout English gentleman was and what had brought him to their remote homeland. They seemed to be mildly amused by the 'orang putih' (white person) in the boat, looking oddly resplendent in a spotless white linen suit, a matching Panama hat and a gaily loud cravat. When he stood up, a servant boy handed him his leather briefcase and his silver-mounted walking cane. He looked like a Kiplingesque colonial, strait out of 'Kim'. Perhaps the older Penans imagined he must be a returning White Rajah.

As the burly English gentleman was about to disembark, he seemed to stumble and fall back headlong into the boat, where he lay writhing upon the bilge, in obvious distress. It was not an accident, however. It was a deliberate attempt on his life by a person hidden from view in the surrounding mangrove thicket. Clearly, that person was an expert marksman, skilled in killing game with his long bamboo blowpipe. Reynolds was struck on the chest by a dart steeped in the deadly venom of a king cobra, the most poisonous snake on the planet. He was rushed to the clinic in Marudi, where he lay on his back, raving, for several hours, his eyes glaring horribly. In that remote station there was no anti-snakebite serum nor any means of contacting the emergency services in Miri and so he died a slow and painful death.

The authorities assumed that the killer was Manser, skulking in the jungle, beyond the reach of the law and there was an intensive police sweep to locate him but he was never found. The next day, something very odd happened. A photo of the Penan group standing on the pier awaiting the arrival of Mr. Reynolds was posted on the Internet. The picture was rather fuzzy but in it, at the rear, one could see what appeared to be a Chinese female. It did not show her features at all clearly but her body shape and attire seemed to indicate that she was Chinese. On hearing of the incident, the police chief in Miri, Kasim Abas, contacted me and begged me to assist in the tracking down the killer. I was puzzled by the photograph and I wondered what the rationale behind its posting on the Internet could be. It was most curious. Clearly, that unseen person was not the killer. She may have been one of Manser's fellow travellers. Saving the rainforest had become a major issue in many parts of Borneo. I might add that it is an issue that we in MI6 fully understand and support but, of course, we would never condone murder.

On seeing the photo, I was most perplexed. The more I looked at it, the more convinced I became that it was a young Chinese female and I wondered who she might be and what she was doing there on the jetty and why the photo had been posted on the internet. I felt that there was something very odd going on – perhaps it was posted on purpose in order to distract attention from the hidden hand of the killer who was probably a Penan hunter skilled in the use of the deadly blowpipe. Obviously, if the police could catch that Penan sharp-shooter, the mystery would be solved. However, catching a Penan in the dense jungle was about as realistic as finding a needle in the proverbial haystack. The police knew that even a cursory sweep of the area would be too dangerous to undertake. It was best to make a hasty retreat to the safety of Miri. As the police chief, Kasim Abas said: 'You do not mess with head-hunting tribal warriors. You could end up in the soup!' And he was not speaking figuratively.

On my return to Kuching, I was surprised that news of the killing of Mr. Reynolds was not mentioned by the Sarawak Chinese. Perhaps they did not wish to be actively involved in a confrontation over logging. In Chinese culture, some things are not talked about and in any case, as Mr. Naylor would say, western people cannot really penetrate the inscrutable oriental mind.

5
THE STINGING SPIDER

A few days after the Marudi incident, I received a call from the police chief in Kuching, Datuk Syed Hamid, informing me that another British subject had died in dubious circumstances in Sarawak - this time in Sibu. He had no details of the matter at that time and advised me to contact the police chief there and make my way to the town, which is much visited by tourists to Sarawak. It is the gateway to the mighty Rajang River and the enchanting rainforest that tourists want to see. Sibu is the ideal starting point for a trip into the heart of Borneo. Most of the residents are Foochow Chinese who settled there in 1901 and most of the indigenous people living in Sibu District are Iban and Melanau.

Nature lovers flock to Sarawak in ever increasing numbers each year to explore it vast rainforest which is a magical world - a paradise for naturalists. It is a vast ecosystem comprising hundreds of subsidiary ecosystems. Its ancient trees and undergrowth are home to all manner of mammals including the chattering gibbons and orangutans – the bronze-red apes with the big eyes and sad faces that everyone loves. On a good day the visitor is likely to see a kaleidoscope of exotic butterflies, including the Rajah Brooke's Birdwing as well as several species of hornbill. However, one has to tread carefully in the rainforest as there are many dangerous creatures lurking in the long grass, for instance, venomous snakes, scorpions, stinging spiders and colonies of pestilential red ants.

It was not only the allure of the rainforest that brought Mary Lou Collins to Sarawak. She is a noted British novelist, specialising in historical fiction. I must confess that I am an avid reader of that genre, which goes beyond the bare facts of textbook history. It takes you behind the great events and the great personages of recorded history to reveal the human aspects of life at that time. For me, it brings history alive and it connects the reader with the past.

Miss Collins was exceptionally good at capturing the 'white dilemma' in British India. I enjoyed reading her two novels on the British Raj. According to the 'London Review of Books' she is one of the best novelists writing historical fiction. She had come to Sarawak to collect source material for a work she was writing on the White Rajahs (the Brookes) who ruled Sarawak for 105 years from 1841 to 1946. As she travelled about in the footsteps of the Brookes, she found that they were loved and hated in equal measure by the local people. She herself was of the view that the White Rajahs had achieved great success in bringing law and order to a lawless land, which they acquired in progressive chunks, beginning with the small district around Kuching and gradually extending it right up to the border of present-day Brunei. The underlying thesis in all her novels is that the British Empire had brought good governance and civility to the coloured races of Africa, India and Southeast Asia. In the subcontinent, the Raj had acted as an honest broker keeping the warring factions apart. It had given British India, Burma and the Straits Settlements an effective civil service, roads, railways, schools and hospitals. It could be construed from her books that the colonised people in the subcontinent and in Southeast Asia were better off under British rule than under their present post-colonial rulers. Her most recent novel on Queen Victoria caused dismay among historians but was warmly applauded by the reading public. In it, she states her unstinting admiration for the great Queen, who like Alexander the Great, ruled over a vast empire on which the sun never set. Personally, I reject her contention that colonisation was good for the colonised.

Of course, before sitting down to write her next historical novel on the Brooke dynasty, she did what all good writers do – she went to the country concerned, in this case Sarawak, to familiarise herself with its history, its topography and, most of all, to get the personal viewpoint of the 'natives'. She was hoping that she would uncover supporting data for her thesis that Sarawak under the White Rajahs was a land of peace and harmony. In fact, she seemed to suggest that the various races of Sarawak would love their country to revert to its former just rule under the British flag.

Miss Collins fell in love with Kuching from the moment her plane landed. On arrival, she bought a copy of Peter Anderson's guidebook to Borneo and Sarawak and it was her constant companion as she explored Kuching, which is one of the most appealing and sophisticated cities in Asia. She stayed at the Kuching Hilton overlooking the Sarawak River. From her balcony she could see across the river Fort Margherita and the Astana, the former palace of the White Rajahs. Of course, she would visit many of the other historical landmarks in the city but her primary focus was the Brooke Gallery in Fort Margherita, which chronicles the story of the White Rajahs and provides copious historical documents, objects, photographs and mementos of that illustrious family, who thanks to the generosity of the Sultan of Brunei, was given ownership of Sarawak. Her admiration for the Brookes was unbounded. She was a little nervous, however, about venturing deep into the rainforest, which is the abode of dangerous reptiles and animals, not to mention the fearsome Iban headhunters.

Before setting out on a trip into the interior, she was shocked when the doorman at the hotel said 'Mind you head, madam. Dem is a bad lot.' He was referring to the Orang Ulu – the wild upriver people who lived in the interior. His name was Jacob and he too was an Iban but not one of the 'wild men of Borneo' clad in bark-cloth with hornbill feathers in their hair; he was a modern educated Iban who, thanks to the White Rajah, had attended St. Thomas' Mission School and learned to read was write in both Iban and English. He added: 'We miss the Brookes so much. They gave us English and the Bible and education.' His endorsement of the White Rajahs was music to her ears. She needed to collect that kind of validation of her subject as she made her way around the country. Having collected all the Kuching data she needed, she then travelled to Sibu, another Brooke location.

Miss Collins found Sibu an enchanting place. She sensed that it was very much a Chinese town, neat and tidy like Singapore and dominated by the impressive seven-storey pagoda. She was keen to explore the town since it was founded by James Brooke in 1862. He built a fort there to protect the white settlers and the Chinese from attacks by the head-hunting Dayaks. The town bears testimony to its colonial past with its wide streets with English names, its churches and temples, its two busy wharfs and its colourful wooden shop-houses. Thanks to tourism, timber and sago, it is a very wealthy town with more millionaires than Singapore. She stayed in the Kingwood Hotel, overlooking the majestic Rajang River. She found the hotel staff most gracious and accommodating but the hotel itself was a bit fayed at the edges. The carpet in her room was threadbare and the wallpaper had begun peeling. The front desk was managed by an elderly but charming Foochow lady, Wendy Foong, who spoke English, in addition to Chinese and Malay. She was the sort of person that Miss Collins was keen to meet since she knew everything about the White Rajahs, even details of their private lives. She recorded much of Wendy's observations and comments in her notebook. As far as she was concerned it was gold dust – the stuff that every writer seeks but seldom finds.

It was Wendy who advised Miss Collins to take a trip down the Rajang River into the rainforest. She should take the express boat to Kapit followed by an overland four-wheel drive through the jungle including a visit to an Iban longhouse. 'Do be careful dear,' she said 'there are lots of dangerous reptiles in the rainforest, not to mention 'hantu' - the spirits and ghosts that dwell there.' Miss Collins knew about 'hantu'. She had been reading a copy of 'The Malaysian Book of the Undead' by Danny Lim in the hotel lobby. She noted that if you upset the hantu by speaking loudly, playing music or urinating under a tree without permission, they would become furious and wreak havoc.

Miss Collins found her trip up the Rajang River an exhilarating experience. The boat, with a dozen tourists on board, set off at 9 a.m. The idea was to reach Kapit by midday. Most of the passengers were German tourists. They passed many huge crocodiles bobbing about like great logs in the muddy water and beyond the river was a vast sago swamp where semi-naked Ibans were busy harvesting the crop. They took pictures of clusters of longhouses perched precariously along both banks of the peat-black river. To European eyes it was another world, exotic and mysterious. On reaching Kapit, they had lunch in the town, which Miss Collins told them was founded by the Second Rajah, Charles Brooke, in 1880. He had a fort built there to protect the settlers from the marauding Orang Ulu. After lunch, they were transported to an Iban longhouse where they consumed several glasses of tauk (rice wine). Then, the inebriated tourists were happy to buy superb Iban artwork, especially rosewood carvings, beaded garments and magnificent paintings of rainforest sights. It was wonderful to see how a large community of Iban managed to live together in harmony, existing off the fruits of the forest and the bounty of the Rajang River.

When Miss Collins returned to her hotel later that day, she had a pleasant surprise. An unknown person had left some fruit for her in a brown paper bag. She assumed it was a gift from someone familiar with her novels. She shook the bag, not knowing what was inside it.

'Rambutans!' exclaimed Wendy. 'Sibu is famous for its rambutans.' Not wishing to appear ignorant, Miss Collins did not ask what rambutans were. Instead, she asked: 'May I know who the donor is?' Wendy told her that she had no idea. She said that people often left messages and packages for clients. With that, Miss Collins went to her room. She guessed that the gift was some kind of fruit. It seems that when she opened the bag, a large spider leaped out and bit her on the forearm. Almost instantly she became queasy and lay on the bed. Her whole body seemed to be consumed with fire and she could barely breathe. She picked up the telephone and in a trembling voice requested immediate medical help. Wendy at once sent one of the maids to Miss Collins' room and told the manager, Mr. Lim to call Dr. Ontong. When he arrived, he found Miss Collins lying on the bed, already in a comatose state. On the fleshy part of her forearm, he noticed an area of swollen tissue where the spider had bitten. He was no stranger to snake and insect bites and almost by instinct he lanced the swollen area, pressed it vigorously between both hands in order to extract the venom. As he was operating, Wendy and the manager arrived and stood in horror at the sight unfolding before their eyes. Being a good Methodist, Wendy fell on knees and began praying for a successful outcome. Sadly, her prayer was not answered. The venom was fatal and there was nothing more Dr. Ontong could do. Before leaving the room, he found the culprit under a pillow – the deadly funnel-web spider which is regarded as the world's most dangerous arachnid. Its bite is ten times more venomous than that of the black widow. It can kill in 15 minutes. It is very rare in Borneo.

'Most curious,' he remarked. 'This species is never found in houses. It lives in the forest, in crevices between the rocks or in holes in trees'. On hearing those words, Wendy almost fainted. She knew that the spider must have been in the bag of rambutans. She would inform the manager of that fact presently and it was up to him to decide how much or how little should be said on the matter. Meanwhile, Dr. Ontong asked for a clean jam jar with a screw-on lid. He caught the spider in his forceps and deposited it in the jar.

'I shall send this evil little devil to the lab for a fuller investigation but I am pretty sure it is the funnel-web spider.' Before leaving he called the coroner and he told the manager to inform the police. It was a sad day for all concerned. Poor Miss Collins had gone to her eternal rest and her novel on the White Rajahs would never be written.

News travels fast in Sarawak. On hearing of the sudden demise of Miss Collins, I left post-haste for Sibu. On arrival at the hotel, I discovered that the victim's body had been removed to the morgue awaiting the coroner's post-mortem. I decided that I should report to the local police chief, Sergeant Omar Yusof, who greeted me warmly and assured me that there was nothing that he or his men could have done to prevent 'this sad misadventure'. He said that it was most regrettable that Miss Collins had been bitten by a poisonous spider. I then pointed out that the killer spider was in the fruit left for Miss Collins and that it may have been deliberately planted.

'Oh yes, of course, we have not ruled out that possibility,' Sergeant Omar replied. 'We have been to the hotel, spoken to the manager and the receptionist and noted their account of the incident. You may want to speak to them yourself in case, as you suggest, it may be more than a horrid misadventure.

On our way to the hotel Sergeant Omar made it clear to me that even if there was circumstantial evidence that the spider had been planted in the rambutans, the matter should not be made public. He would conduct a thorough investigation and do his utmost to discover the whereabouts of the fruit donor – the young lady that nobody had seen entering or leaving the hotel. On one point he was most adamant. Even if it was found that Miss Collins had been killed by an unknown person, it would serve no useful purpose to have that fact made public. The perpetrator would be tracked down and charged with capital murder. In due course, he or she would be tried and if found guilty, they would spend 40 years in prison. All of that would happen under the radar and nobody would be the wiser. It was pointless announcing that the victim had been murdered as it would compound the grief of the Collins family back in the UK. Moreover, it would have a grave detrimental impact on the economy of Sibu and especially the tourist industry. The Governor of the Sibu Division had that morning ordered the police chief not to divulge any information about the affair to the media. The hotel staff had also been warned to remain tight-lipped about it. If asked about the spider, everyone was to explain that unfortunately accidents happen, especially in Sibu which is surrounded by dangerous reptiles and insects.

On arrival at the hotel, I was warmly welcomed by the manager, Mr. Lim, whom the police chief had instructed not to say more than the bare facts of the case and to make it clear that poisonous spiders, scorpions and snakes tend to kill people and animals.

'No doubt you will want to speak to our receptionist, Miss Foong. She was on duty on the evening of the mishap. Please feel free to use my office,' he said. Lim's use of the word 'mishap' seemed to be an attempt on his part to avoid any suggestion of foul play. All of us in MI6 know that words are revelatory. We pay attention to word choice as well as tone of voice and intonation. We are trained to detect misinformation at every crime location.

Wendy Foong found herself torn on the horns of a dilemma. She was obliged to reject any suggestion of willful murder while at the same time keeping intact her Methodist morality. The words 'tragic accident' seemed appropriate in the situation. 'Yes, God knows it was a tragic accident,' she told me.

'But it may not have been an accident,' I suggested. 'Perhaps somebody wanted to get rid of Miss Collins.'

'Oh, no!' exclaimed Miss Foong. 'That is sheer fantasy. Miss Collins had no enemies here. We welcome tourists with open arms. We need tourists. Why should anyone have her killed?'

'Well, some people in Southeast Asia might not agree with her views on merits of colonisation and especially her contention that the native people were better off under British rule,' I replied. 'The Raj was not quite as benign as she makes out in her novels. You will recall that the White Rajahs ruled Sarawak for a hundred year from 1841 to 1946. As in India, British Malaya and British Borneo were systematically robbed of their resources. In Southeast Asia, the Chinese especially were badly treated and had to endure a hundred years of colonial misrule and exploitation. Your people, the Chinese, might not take kindly to being told they were better off under British rule. I understand there is still considerable anti-British feeling in Sibu. You may recall that the second British Governor of Sarawak, Sir Duncan Stewart, was assassinated in Sibu in 1949. We cannot ignore the past.'

'That may be so,' conceded Miss Foong, 'but we all got a good education under the British. I should not say this but in some ways our present government is much worse than the British ever were. I know many of us here in Sibu would prefer the White Rajahs any day to the 'bandits' that came after them.'

I was shocked at Miss Foong's candid comments and not wishing to go down the road of post-colonial recrimination, I asked her to recall her meeting with the donor of the rambutans. She said it was a brief encounter, perhaps less than two or three minutes. She had been checking in a client at the time and she had not paid much attention to the young lady who suddenly entered the reception area, placed a brown paper bag on the counter, and said: 'A small gift for Miss Collins.' She went on: 'That was all she said. She spoke to me in Hokkien. Then she left as briskly as she had entered. I noticed that the words 'For Miss Collins' were written on the bag. The young lady was quite tall and good looking. She was wearing a helmet and a black leather jacket. I should point out that people often leave messages and gifts for visitors, so there was nothing unusual in that. Later, that evening, when Miss Collins and the others arrived back from their boat trip down the Rajang River, I gave her the gift. She seemed pleasantly surprised. She shook the bag, not knowing what was in it. 'Rambutans!' I told her. That was all. She went to her room and I have no idea what transpired there. I have been told that when she opened the bag, a spider leaped out and bit her on the forearm. That bite, it seems, was fatal.'

I felt that Miss Foong knew more than she was saying and that she was reluctant to divulge any useful information about the mysterious young lady who had delivered the fruit. I asked her if she saw that person again could she identify her.

'Probably not,' she replied. 'As I have told you, she is quite tall, slim and obviously Chinese. She may have come on a motorcycle since she was wearing a helmet and black leather gloves.'

Later that morning, I paid a visit to Dr. Ontong, who confirmed that Miss Collins was already in a comatose state when he arrived and that she was 'hanging on to life' as he put it.

'Sadly, there is no antidote for the deadly bite of the funnel-web spider. Its venom, like that of the black mamba, attacks the nervous system and causes asphyxia. What I find really perplexing is how that spider got into the hotel. That species is extremely rare in Sarawak. Only a few samples have been sighted and recorded. Moreover, they are never found in buildings. Their habitat is the rainforest. Most peculiar, in my opinion,' he said in a very puzzled tone of voice.

Before leaving Sibu, I went to see Sergeant Omar at the Balai Police Station. We discussed the sad demise of Miss Collins. He seemed convinced that it was 'a sad misadventure' – a tragic accident that happens occasionally in the tropical rainforest, where all manner of poisonous reptiles and insects abound.

'It is fate' he said, 'and we should not assume that evil spirits are abroad, killing innocent people'. He also indicated that the Governor of Sibu Province, Chief Jonathan, would be most annoyed at any suggestion of foul play. Of course, the Sibu police would continue to track down the mysterious young lady who delivered the rambutans.

He said that leaving a gift as a token of appreciation for a person of note was not a crime in Sarawak!

'One should not read too much into such an event,' he went on 'Lots of people here have a high regard for Miss Collins and her splendid novels. In my humble opinion, she's probably the best oriental novelist since Maugham.' He pointed out that the only material evidence he had managed to obtain was the bag of rambutans and of course a dead spider, now in the police lab. I then asked to see the bag on which the fruit donor had written 'For Miss Collins.' I said that if he had no objection, I would send it to London and have the writing analysed by a graphologist. I pointed out that the written word might be as good as a fingerprint or a footprint. As I left the station, Sergeant Omar said: 'In our line of business, we tend to see evil where it does not exist. However, accidents happen. People get bitten by spiders and snakes quite often here in Sarawak.' He then suggested that I should visit Sibu more often since in his words it is 'a very civilised place' and its people are peace-loving and law-abiding, adding: 'You see, the age of head-hunting is but a distant memory'. However, I felt that there was something sinister about the whole affair. As old Mr. Naylor in MI5 used to say: 'A good secret agent should be able to smell a rat a mile away.' There were plenty of rats in the storm drains of Sibu; however, he was obviously not referring to rodents but to people of criminal intent.

REMEMBERING THINGS PAST

On my return to Kuching, I spent some time wondering what the great detective Sherlock Holmes would have made of the 'tragic accident' in Sibu about which my informants seemed reluctant to speak. In my mind, it was too simplistic to blame it all on a venomous spider. However, the key person in the event – the young Chinese lady bearing the gift – had disappeared without a trace. The golden rule in crime detection is to look for a possible motive. After all, everything happens for a reason. I had to ask myself what prompted somebody in Sarawak to resort to killing visiting British subjects. Perhaps the killer was motivated by political discontent arising from colonial history. We know that the British, the Spanish and the Dutch had occupied the greater part of Southeast Asia for centuries. We also know that colonials were instinctively racist and regarded coloured people as inferior to them. Moreover, we know that several legacy issues remain unresolved today in many former colonies of the great British Empire.

Things were not going well for us in MI6. The mysterious killing of three prominent British subjects – Sir Basil Green, Mr. Colin Reynolds and Mary Lou Collins by an unknown person residing somewhere in Sarawak had by now created a good deal of apprehension not only in Sarawak but across Southeast Asia. British expatriates living and working in the region began to fear for their safety. The British press had a field day, castigating MI6 and the Malaysian Special Branch for gross incompetence. The Daily Dispatch was especially venomous, saying 'our man in Kuching is being outwitted by a nameless Chinese dragon'. Naturally, my boss was not amused and I was told to 'nail the bitch before she nails you.'

I trawled through the confidential Home Office files on each of the victims. I soon discovered that Sir Basil was known to have been a serial sex offender with a fondness for slim oriental women. Perhaps his killer intended to avenge his lustful exploits in Kuching and beyond. However, he had no known criminal connections. As for the racist Mr. Reynolds, several reports listed his xenophobic outbursts and hate speech. It seemed fairly obvious to me that he was bound to be a marked man in a country which still implemented race-based politics and turned a blind eye to the rape of the rainforest at the expense of the indigenous people. The novelist Miss Collins was not mentioned at all. I assumed that she may have been targeted because she was too kindly disposed to the White Rajahs who ruled Sarawak for over a hundred years. As I travelled across the region from Sarawak, to Brunei, Labuan, Sabah, Malacca, Penang, Selangor and Singapore I discovered that there was a good deal of discontent in Paradise. All the diverse races – the Malays, the Chinese, the Indians, the Indonesian and Pakistani migrant workers, and the indigenous people complained of blatant discrimination on racial or religious grounds.

I shall not dwell on our dismal colonial rule in the Straits Settlements since I am not a historian. The history of the region is well documented by Professor D.G.E. Hall (1955) in *History of Southeast Asia* which I carry with on my travels. It tells how the two great powers, the British and the Dutch, had carved up the Malay Archipelago into two separate spheres of influence. Penang, Malacca and Singapore were assigned to Britain and known as the Straits Settlements while the territory south of the Straits, namely modern Indonesia, was assigned to the Dutch. Today, many Chinese in the Malay States, Singapore, Sarawak and Sabah have bitter memories of British rule. People in Singapore still remember how Stamford Raffles had established a trading post there in 1819 and how it had grown into a major city as a Crown Colony from 1826 to 1942. They remembered how in 1841 the Sultan of Brunei had ceded Sarawak to James Brooke, who was proclaimed Rajah and Governor of Sarawak. They remembered with scorn how the Sultan of Sulu had ceded sovereignty of Sabah to Alfred Dent of the British North Borneo Chartered Company. Were the Chinese or the Malays consulted about all of that land-grabbing? Of course not. In the colonial mind-set they were an inferior race whose existence was tolerated as second-class citizens. In a book about mining in Malaya, the writer Warnford-Lock (1907) expresses the rampant racism of the ruling elite: 'By nature, the Malay is an idler, the Chinaman is a thief and the Indian is a drunkard. Yet each, in his special class of work is both cheap and efficient when properly supervised.'

We know that waves of Chinese migrated to British Malaya during the 19th century. They found work in the gold and tin mines in the Kinta Valley and in rubber plantations in Malacca. Later, they opened shop-houses and restaurants in the towns. They continued to expand and prosper and today they dominate the business and commercial sections of the Malaysian economy. They currently form 25% of the population. The Malays are known as 'bumiputras' (sons of soil) and they enjoy affirmative action on all fronts. Some of the more fundamentalist Muslim MPs in Putrajaya dislike and distrust the Chinese, especially those who are Christian. They see them as a threat to their Islamic culture. Chinese intellectuals often complain about the greed, endemic corruption, institutional racism and race-based politics of the BN government but many Chinese business people do not complain at all. The manager of my local pub in Kuching, Mr. Tan told me: 'Of course the Malays are corrupt, but we always win because we are more corrupt than them.' He was joking of course!

The main bone of contention in Malaysia at that time was the Constitution which was drafted in 1957 by Professor Hugh Hickling, a colonial lawyer. Many of its provisions are quite liberal, for instance, it stipulates equality to all, no discrimination on the ground of race, religion, descent, gender or place of birth. It also stipulates freedom of religion and freedom of assembly. However, Article 149 stipulates 'special powers for parliament against subversion, organized violence and acts and crimes prejudicial to the public.' That provision gave the ruling BN government special powers to arrest and charge members of the opposition with subversion, sedition or 'Islamic offences'. It gave them licence to crush all political opponents in ways which Hickling had never envisaged. The Constitution states that the Federation of Malaysia is a secular state and Article 153 affirms 'affirmative action' to safeguard the special position of the Malay 'bumiputras' (sons of the soil). That article caused a good deal of grief since it contradicted the 'equality to all' provision and was used by the BN to retain power. Thus, loyal Muslim supporters in the kampungs (villages) got the best schools, clinics, housing and other benefits while the non-Muslims got very little. Worse was to follow. The draconian Internal Security Act (1960), drafted by Professor Hickling, was enacted to combat insurgency, terrorism and subversion. Under ISA, many innocent people were arrested and sent to a Detention Centre in Perak, where they were routinely beaten and tortured. In other words, the ISA was used by the ruling BN coalition to silence and suppress political opponents, human rights campaigners, media bloggers and any persons deemed to be enemies of the state. At that time, Malaysia was regarded globally as a very corrupt and a very flawed democracy under the monstrous misrule of the BN government, which Dean Johns (2011: 132) has described as follows: 'Like every other people-robbing government, Malaysia's BN regime supports its thievery with a system of corruption, repression, secrecy, lies and low cunning.' However, I know that things are different now. Malaysia has moved on and it is no longer a repressive state.

The situation in Singapore was quite different. That small city-state, established as a trading post under the East India Company in 1819, came under British colonial rule in 1857 and later became a British Crown colony. On gaining independence, it joined the Malay Federation in 1963 and two years later declared full independence. Today, it is a very prosperous and civilised place. It has the highest concentration of Chinese in Southeast Asia - 75% of its population. Many of its people enjoy a very high standard of living. Its schools and universities are second to none. It is virtually crime-free. It is the only city in Southeast Asia where you will not be ripped off by a taxi driver. Most of the Singaporeans I know seem reasonably happy with the status quo. However, the younger generation sometimes voice criticism of the dogmatism of its rulers. They also dislike the tendency of its elder citizens to ape British manners, attitudes and British RP pronunciation. They use Singlish quite a lot in casual conversation. The millennials see themselves as 'more Chinese than the Chinese' and they want closer ties with Mother China. The modern tendency of softening towards the 'motherland and its culture', i.e., the People's Republic is something that concerns us in MI6 and the Foreign Office. We simply cannot afford to let the Peoples' Republic push us out of Singapore.

Sabah, the 'Land Below the Wind', has become a major tourist mecca in the region. I have been there several times and climbed the famous Mount Kinabalu towering above the city of Kota Kinabalu (KK). Sabah is an enormous state but it has a small population of 3.5 million. It has great natural beauty – pristine beaches, exotic islands, coral reefs, rainforest and abundant wildlife. The state has a long colonial history. It was acquired by the North Borneo Chartered Company in 1882. It was occupied by the Japanese for three years during World War 2 and it became a British Crown colony in 1946. In 1963, it decided to join the Federation of Malaysia. There are three main indigenous communities – the Kadasan, Dusun and Murut, which are said to have originated from South China but they are quite distinct from the Chinese, who comprise about 10% of the population. Almost everyone I met there voiced discontent over government policy. They claimed that their Islamic rulers subscribed to the concept of Malay Islamic Monarchy (MIB) and turned a blind eye to illegal immigration from Sulu, Indonesia and Pakistan in order to boost the Muslim population. During my last visit I got the impression that the ship of state was floundering in a sea of discontent.

Finally, a few words about my favourite place in Southeast Asia, Brunei, which is known as the 'Abode of Peace.' Oil-rich Brunei used to be a British Protectorate and its ruler, Sultan Hassanal Bolkiah, maintains close ties with the UK. He is an absolute monarch. In fact, he owns the country and he is reported to be the richest monarch in the world. He lives in a splendid palace which is bigger than Buckingham Palace; it has 1,800 rooms. His Majesty has a fondness for works of art, classic cars and polo, while his offspring enjoy flying about in private

Boeing jet planes. The Sultanate still exhibits a classic three-tier feudal structure. At the top of the pyramid are the C1 class - the Sultan and his nobles, the so-called 'pengirans.' Below them are the C2 class – the ordinary Bruneians and the permanent residents, most of whom are Chinese. The Chinese are not allowed to own land but may operate a business in conjunction with a 'sleeping partner' from the elite C1 class. At the bottom of the pile are the C3 class - the indigenous people, most of whom live in the Temburong District. They are the landless native people who retain their own tribal language, customs and way of life.

I did not encounter much discontent among the people there. However, a few Chinese complained of racial discrimination. They pointed out that many ethnic Chinese have lived in Brunei for generations and amount to 15% of the population. However, they remain stateless permanent residents and not citizens. One's entitlement to government services (health care, education, social welfare, grants, etc.) depend on the colour of your national identity card. Ethnic Brunei citizens have a yellow IC while ethnic Chinese permanent residents have a purple IC.

A lot of British, Australian and New Zealand expatriates live and work in Brunei. One English language teacher in BSB told me: 'The problem with living in Brunei is the red tape. Your life is not your own. You cannot travel or leave the country without permission. You cannot employ an amah (housemaid) without permission. You cannot enroll your children in a school or college without permission. You spend hours every week in the Establishment Building seeking permission for all sorts of trivial matters.' He went on to tell us about a lady whose husband had died in Brunei. Before returning home to New Zealand, she had to close her husband's various accounts and she went along to the Electricity Department to do that. However, the officer in charge told her that it was impossible. The account had to be closed by the same person who opened it. 'But my husband has died,' she said 'and we are returning to New Zealand.' The official still insisted that the account could not be closed because the person who opened it 'had died without permission'!

However, expatriates live quite happily in Brunei in spite of its sclerotic rules. It is a little gem of a country. Obviously, the young people would like more social freedom and less red tape. However, their criticism of the government is muted and so it should be since Brunei is one of the few countries in the world in which all workers are exempt from income tax and are entitled to free health care, free schooling, subsidised housing and all modern amenities. The best thing about Brunei is the rainforest. It is simply stunning especially in the Temburong District.

Now, having outlined a rough guide of the territory in which MI6 operates, it is time to return to my special assignment in Sarawak. While in Sibu I got the impression that the local police were treating the death of Miss Collins as 'unexplained'. The police chief confirmed that his men had not submitted a report on their interrogation of the hotel staff where Miss Collins met her death. When asked why that was the case, he said that they had 'run out of pencils.'

Clearly, the local police were facing a very unusual crime which might have political implications and that is why they asked MI6 to assist in tracking down the killer. However, solving a crime is like doing a jigsaw puzzle; each piece adds to the picture. Clearly, it is never easy when most of the pieces are missing. So far, all we had on the suspect were a few tiny fragments of evidence; not a single piece of significant evidence. No fingerprints. No blood on the carpet. No DNA.

Bonner-Davies and I speculated that it may have been political discontent that motivated the mysterious killer that we were seeking. She may have felt that Chinese identity and culture had been suppressed for too long in Southeast Asia and she may have seen herself as a latter-day liberator for her race, possibly walking in the footsteps of her hero, Chin Peng. All of that, of course, was pure speculation on our part. For no particular reason, Kipling's poem, *The White Man's Burden* (1899) came to mind. In it, he proposes that the white man is morally obliged to civilize the non-white people of the world. It is a poem in praise of white imperialism and colonisation. Students of history know very well that the past is never past. We are all shaped by our history. Instances of oppression and misrule are indelibly inscribed in the collective consciousness of people. It is the memory of past domination and exploitation that inspires freedom fighters to take up arms against an oppressive regime, possibly leading to 'rivers of blood'. That is something that we in MI6 do our best to forestall.

7

THE GREEN MIST

I was scarcely back in Kuching when my phone rang and our man in Sandakan, in a very agitated tone of voice, informed me that a 'serious situation' had arisen and that my presence was urgently required. I was naturally taken aback at this sudden and unexpected development. I had already booked the Waterfront Hotel in Labuan where I was looking forward to a few days of peaceful relaxation. Of course, in MI6 the motto is 'expect the unexpected'. In our line of business, when duty calls, one has to respond. I assumed that the 'serious situation' most likely involved the incursion of a band of brigands from Sulu. They were well known to us in MI6 as Abu-Sayaf, a kidnap-for-ransom organisation affiliated to the Moro Liberation Front on the Sulu Islands. The east coast of Sabah had previously been part of the Sulu empire and the Moro Liberation Front still claimed ownership of the territory. Their modus operandi was to arrive in speed boats, seize a prominent and wealthy person and demand ransom, otherwise the person in question would be shot and end up in the South China Sea. The last thing the government wanted was bloodshed; the raiders were paid and made off in haste before a naval force could blockade them. For several years the east coast of Sabah had been the focus of such strange doings. MI6 had repeatedly requested the UK government to provide Sabah with gun ships and helicopters but the Secretary for Defence decided that Britain no longer had the financial resources to protect the coasts of every country in the free world. Britain was no longer a great power.

Fortunately, I was able to catch a midday flight to Sandakan and Myles Brogan, our man there, was waiting for me at the airport. He said: 'We're in a spot of bother right now. Let's not hang about. Sandakan is no longer a safe place.'

'It never was,' I replied. 'I suspect that our bearded friends from Sulu are up to their old tricks. 'Wrong assumption,' he barked 'It's something rather more sinister I'm afraid. Does the name Sir Giles Roper mean anything to you?' he asked.

'Yes, isn't he a member of the State Assembly?' Brogan looked at me askance and said: 'He used to be.'

'Is he not well or in trouble?' I asked, to which he replied. 'Worse still, he's dead. The police here suspect that he was killed at by an unseen hand and as usual they have asked us to help them track down the killer.

Brogan suggested that we proceed at once to the police chief, Datuk Hamza Sharbini for a briefing on the case. On the way, he informed me that there had been a disturbance in the main square the previous day after which Sir Giles fled to the safety of his villa. As he was getting into his car, he was accosted by unknown person who seemed to spray a green mist in Sir Giles' face. Several people had seen the green mist but nobody had seen the dispensing hand or the person's face.

When we arrived at police headquarters, we were told that Datuk Hamza was out and would not be back until after lunch. That being the case, we decided to have lunch in a small Chinese café called 'Jacob's Den'. Over lunch, Brogan put me in the picture, so to speak, regarding the unrest in region. He told me that the situation was pregnant with wild rumours and much discontent. In spite of Sabah's great natural resources 20% of the population were living below the poverty line. Most of the money from the sale of petroleum, natural gas, rice and timber was going into deep pockets in Kuala Lumpur and only about 5% of the revenue Sabah generated was trickling back into the state coffers. As in Sarawak, vast areas of native rainforest had been acquired by multi-national syndicates and were being cleared for the cultivation of palm oil with devastating consequences for biodiversity. Of course, none of that information was news to me. The rape of the rainforest was well known. Foreign mining companies were operating all over the state and offshore drilling companies were busy extracting oil and natural gas with the connivance of the Federal government. Naturally, the Sabahans were not amused and there were street protests by disgruntled farmers and the ulu people who lived in the rainforest. On hearing of the discontent, the inner circle in Kuala Lumpur became alarmed and decided to launch a counter offensive. The Federal Minister for Rural Development contacted his old friend Sir Giles Roper advising him to reassure the residents of the Eastern province that their traditional lands would be protected. Everyone would share in the economic development of the region. All land taken over for mining and logging would be compensated in full. The government was about to launch a whole raft of social welfare benefits, subsidised housing, a free state medical service, hospitals, schools and all necessary infrastructure. Soon Sabah would be as prosperous as Singapore.

Sir Giles lost no time in spreading the word and arranged consultation sessions with various bodies in Sandakan, Lahad Datu, Semporna and Tawau. He then called for a public meeting in the main square of Sandakan at which he spent much time explaining the new 'One Malaysia' policy under which all member states of the Federation would share in the country's prosperity and no state would be left behind. He was an impressive public speaker fluent in English, Malay and Chinese. He stated that he was a special adviser to the Minister for Rural Development and that his recommendations would be acted upon. However, the crowd was restless and a small group barracked him with cries of 'Enough of corruption! Land grabbers out! Sabah for Sabahans!' It soon became apparent that a full-scale riot was about to erupt and Sir Giles sensing the danger, abruptly ended his speech and made for his car which was parked beside the platform. As he descended the steps however, angry protestors pressed forward menacingly and in an instant, a hidden hand was seen spraying a green mist onto his face. The police managed to bundle him into his car which drove off at speed. This disturbance happened so suddenly that nobody was able to identify the culprit. It was said that a hooded woman had been seen in the vicinity but nobody had seen her face nor could they verify that she responsible for the dastardly deed.

We did not return to police headquarters. Instead, the police chief contacted Brogan telling him to proceed to Mount Vernon, the home of Sir Giles on a vast estate overlooking the South China Sea. On the way, Brogan told me about the Roper family whose members were in former times regarded as merchant princes. Sir Giles was the grandson of Charles Roper, who was a close associate of Alfred Dent, the founder of the North Borneo Chartered Company, which acquired the territory and ran it as a private enterprise for sixty-four years from 1882 to 1946. Kudat, at the northern tip of Borneo, was chosen as the capital. Subsequently, the territory was extended along the east coast. Then the whole of Sabah became a British protectorate and was divided into five administrative zones called Residencies, two on the west coast and three on the east coast. The Ropers became Residents and district governors in Sandakan. They became the wealthiest and most powerful family in Sabah. Giles studied law in London, became a barrister and was later elected Member of the Sabah State Assembly. He was special adviser to the Minister for Rural Development. He was said to be a mild-mannered man and a progressive politician. However, few residents of Sandakan had any confidence in his ability to bring prosperity to their area. The indigenous people and the Chinese where all clamouring for an end to endemic corruption and nepotism. As Brogan put it, 'the old ship of state was floundering in a sea of discontent.'

It was not long before we arrived at Mount Vernon, the ancestral home of the Ropers. The gatekeeper opened giant iron-wrought gates and we entered a long driveway flanked by pungent-smelling shrubbery, brightly coloured hibiscus in bloom and lawns banked by swaying bamboos. Mount Vernon is a palatial residence which at first glance reminded me of Du Maurier's Manderley. Built in the Dutch colonial style, the house is characterised by a gambrel roof with curved eaves along the length of the house, woodwork cladding, shuttered windows and a solid teak front door accented by a pediment and classical columns.

We were met and welcomed by the butler who escorted us up a marble stairway to Sir Giles' bedroom on the upper floor. The room was in semi darkness and several gentlemen were standing beside bed including the police chief Datuk Hamza Sharbini. Dr. Namoos, an eminent epidemiologist had already arrived and had conducted a close examination of the body.

'Looks like a poisonous gas, most probably chlorine or something identical. Strong and deadly stuff. The fumes of chlorine can kill an elephant.' He was wearing surgical gloves and through a chemist's mask his voice sounded hoarse.

'Keep your distance,' he said as he rolled back the sheet covering the head of the deceased.

'Good Lord!' was the only expression I could utter at that moment. Before me was a terrible sight, a human head gone green and facial features contorted in obvious pain. The face glowed with a luminescent green sheen. I am no strange to dead bodies and mangled human remains but this was different, really sinister, the white of the victim's bulging eyes contrasting with the green of the surrounding skin.

Then the luminous green body was wrapped in white linen and transported to the morgue where a post-mortem was be conducted. We did not think is appropriate to stay and chat with family members. On the way out, Datuk Hamza assured me that he and his men would track down the culprit. 'Stay in contact,' he said 'we shall conduct a thorough investigation and with the help of Allah we shall apprehend the evil person who did this vile act.'

I had grave doubts about the ability of Datuk Hamza to find the killer. In fact, I knew instinctively that something weird was going on and I was in the thick of it. Another mysterious killing had taken place and we were all in the dark. A secret and malign force was obviously abroad but neither I nor the Sandakan police had the vaguest notion who or what was behind it. I did not relish returning empty handed to my hotel where my immediate task was composing and dispatching a coded cable to the High Commission in KL and my superior at the SIS Building in London giving an account of the day's proceedings. Neither of those recipients were going to be impressed at my dismal failure to hunt down the mysterious angel of death. Datuk Hamza promised to keep me updated on the case and next morning I caught the ferry boat to Labuan.

8

THE GELATINA SPECIALE

One of my favourite places in Southeast Asia is the island of Labuan which has become a major tourist resort. I normally stay at the Waterfront Hotel or the nearby Sheraton where the service and the food are outstanding and where you are likely to meet interesting people from Brunei, Sabah, Sarawak and Singapore. It was there that I first met Edward Summers at the poolside of the Waterfront Hotel. Somehow, Edward stood out from the crowd. He was a brilliant conversationalist and quite a character, with a pronounced Northern accent. He was known as Ed, 'the man from Seria'. He was a senior drilling engineer with Brunei Shell. His job entailed the planning and supervision of drilling offshore operations in designated fields in the South China Sea. He had extensive experience of reservoir modelling and team management working closely with geology, geophysics and drilling teams. He held a Masters Degree in Petroleum Engineering from the University of Leeds and he had previously worked with Aramco in Saudi Arabia. Such men are much sought after by the oil industry and they, unlike me, are paid an enormous tax-free salary.

In the afternoon I went down to the swimming pool where I met several of my old friends and acquaintances. I was surprised that none of them had seen Summers recently and I decided to have a word with the manager, Carlo Gomez.

'I'm afraid it's a rather long story,' he said 'and sadly you will not be seeing Ed again'. He took me to his office and poured me a double whiskey. 'Too bad. I bring bad news. It all happened last week.' Having set the scene, Carlo shared the following story with me. On the previous Friday, Ed was having a beer by the poolside when he noticed a slim raven-haired Chinese beauty queen approaching. She sat under the canopy by the bar and ordered a Martini. She then took out her mobile and spent quite some time responding to messages and chatting. Ed was instantly attracted to her. He hesitated at first, not wishing to appear forward but he soon decided to take the plunge. Perhaps the goddess wished to hook up with a man of substance from oil-rich Brunei.

'Excuse me, miss, but I was wondering what brings you to this desert island.'

'Most likely, the same reason that brings you here' she replied with a smile.

Soon, the two strangers were immersed in conversation as if they were old friends. She said it was her first visit the Labuan which she hoped to explore in the coming days. Ed talked about his work for Brunei Shell in Seria, and more generally about the expatriate community there, where all evil things such as drugs, alcohol and sex were forbidden. Later, they dived into the pool and did several lengths before resting at the lower end. The pool attendant noticed them in close proximity. He claimed that he saw 'the pretty one' throw herself forward, pressing her jeweled hands against his shoulders while looking earnestly into his face with passionate pleading eyes. Suddenly, she took a sip of her Martini and pressing her lips against Ed's, a gush of warm Martini passed from her mouth to his. It was the sort of intimate kiss that one reads about in romantic novels such as 'Madame Bovary', that sort of kiss that drives men insane. The pool attendant turned away in disgust at the sight of two bodies coiled together in an embrace of love.

Later that afternoon Ed and his lady friend had high tea in the hotel restaurant. It was the head waiter who discovered that the lady's name was Amanda and that she was a beauty consultant over from Singapore on a PR mission. He described her as a tall, slim young lady, in a clinging red silk gown embroidered with golden dragon motifs. He added that she looked like a model straight out of Vogue. The meal was a splendid affair. They dined off Coq Au Vin washed down with the best Sauvignon Blanc. The dessert was 'gelatina speciale' – assorted ice cream in a bed of jelly, the invention of the new pastry chef, Ricardo. It tasted divine. Before leaving the restaurant, the head waiter asked Ed if he wished to book a table for dinner that evening but Ed explained that Amanda had to attend a promotion event that evening across the road at the Sheraton Hotel. He had arranged to pick her up later, around 10 p.m. and spend some time in the 'Jupiter Club'. Shortly after that Ed walked Amanda to the Sheraton Hotel and on his return retired to his room on the first floor.

No sooner had he reached his bedroom than he felt unwell. He felt dizzy and his legs began to wobble under him. He felt his head spinning round and he began sweating profusely. He grasped the rim of the wash-hand basin and held on for dear life. He looked in the mirror and saw a puffed-up face staring back at him and small streams of sweat pouring down each side of his face and neck. It seemed to him like the onset of a heart attack and he lay on the bed where he lapsed into a coma from which he never recovered. Next morning, around 10 a.m. the cleaning lady knocked on his door to find out if he wished to have his room attended to but there was no response. She then called the janitor who unlocked the door and to his shock and horror, found Ed dead in his bed.

The manager, Carlo, immediately informed the police and the hotel was declared a crime scene. Nobody was allowed to enter or leave while the police conducted a full-scale investigation. The pool attendants, the waiters, the guests on the same floor and the manager were interrogated and statements were taken. Later that morning the state coroner was flown in from Sabah and he ordered the body to be removed to the morgue and all items belonging to Ed as well as food items were packed and sent to the forensic laboratory in Kuala Lumpur.

Meanwhile a massive manhunt was under way across the island. Every hotel and boarding house were searched but even though all departure points from the island had been closed the young lady called Amanda disappeared without a trace. Alarmingly, the pastry chef

Ricardo had also disappeared. You did not have to be Sherlock Holmes to suspect that somebody had put more than panna in Ed's gelato. Was that person Amanda and was she the 'dragon'? I remember saying to myself: 'My God! Is there no end to the cunning and inventiveness of the lady?'

By midday it was clear that Amanda and her accomplice Ricardo had made good their escape. The police chief surmised that they must have absconded in a speedboat before daybreak and might have landed on one of the offshore islands or possibly even made for Singapore where Amanda supposedly was based. There seemed no other explanation. After all, Labuan is a small island and the only way out is by land or sea and there are no night flights or early morning ferry crossings. I stayed in Labuan for two days helping the police to find clues to the killing. However, we were unable to find any evidential material that would enable us to track her down. Bonner-Davies, my MI6 boss in London, instructed me to make my way to Singapore that weekend in the hope that the mysterious Amanda might show up. The Singapore Special Branch are top drawer and I knew they would search every nook and cranny where a fugitive might be hiding. However, our search was of no avail.

I wondered why the kind and inoffensive Ed Summers had been targeted. It must have been due to his association with Brunei Shell. He was perhaps seen as part and parcel of the greedy western cartel that was robbing Borneo of its natural resources. Once more, I have to confess that such a conclusion was mere conjecture on my part. The other possibility was that she was a very sick psychopath. The only thing I knew with certainty was that catching the elusive 'dragon' would be far from plain sailing. We had no idea where she would pop up next.

9

A SINGAPORE SLING

As I was about to return to Kuching, I had an urgent call from our man in Singapore, Josh Hall. He informed me that there had been a murder of a British subject there. I found that news shocking in view of the fact that Singapore is the most law-abiding state in Southeast Asia; its government and police enforce zero tolerance of crime. The victim this time was a prominent British barrister, Roger Bentham QC, who had been visiting the city on business and suddenly disappeared. MI6 did the usual research on him and forwarded it at once to the Singapore Special Branch, to our High Commissioner and to MI6 in Singapore.

Josh met me at the airport. 'I hope you have a good insurance policy' he said. 'Singapore is no longer a safe place.' He was a jovial person, born and reared in Rangoon where his father was an academic. Like his illustrious father, Josh knew Southeast Asia like the back of his hand and his knowledge of the colonial history of the region was profound. He was also a brilliant linguist, fluent in several Chinese dialects, Singlish, Burmese and Malay.

Josh had showed me a copy of the police file on Rupert Bentham and it certainly made interesting reading. He was the only son of Baroness Beatrix Bentham of Musgrove Manor in Sussex. At Oxford

University, he was known to be gregarious and fond of throwing wild parties at which he is said to have danced naked on the dining table for the entertainment of his guests. He read law at Oxford after which he worked in the legal department of the Foreign and Commonwealth Office at Whitehall. He was often seen entertaining foreign dignitaries at Lancaster House. He made rapid progress, was called to the bar and soon became a noted barrister, specialising in Constitutional Law. In 1970, he was requested by the Federal government in Putrajaya to look over a draft copy of the new Sedition Bill which was being revised. The original Sedition Act (1948) was introduced by the British colonial government to use against communist insurgents. In 1970, its scope was extended so as to silence government critics. And so, he travelled to KL where he set to work. He was in his element. His brief was rather ambiguous. He was asked to deal with the 'infelicities' in the Constitution and to amend the Sedition Act (1948). The government had promised to repeal it but in fact did the opposite. Bentham was instructed to word it in such a way that it sounded less draconian but at the same time would have a wider remit. It would (a) ban any act, speech or publication impugning the character or reputation of the government or Malaysia's nine sultans; (b) ban any act, speech or publication inciting hatred between the different races and religions of the country; (c) ban any questioning of the special position of Islam and the ethnic Malay race – the 'bumiputras'. It was a task that Bentham looked forwarded to with relish. As a result of his intervention, Malaysia spiraled into a dark era of repression. The amended Act was used to conduct a smear campaign against opposition MPs, academics critical of government policy, any non-conforming media people and especially online bloggers, all of whom were branded subversives. The aim was to have a legal instrument to target, arrest and silence all critical voices, and where necessary to have them sent to the Taiping Detention Centre, a prison camp in Perak for 'enemies of the state.'

We were unable to obtain independent verification of Bentham's role in drafting the new provisions. Obviously, the government was not going to divulge the name of the author of the new legislation much less how it was to be enforced. What we do know is that the Sedition Act was amended at the same time that Bentham was in KL. We talked to various media people in KL on this matter and all of them confirmed that the amended Sedition Act had just been published and that its provisions were causing grave concern across the country especially among the Chinese and Indians. However, nobody we spoke to knew who was responsible for drafting it.

Our research department in London discovered that Bentham had been the subject of a police investigation some years previously. It was alleged that he had engaged in sexual harassment of female clients, including sexual advances, requests for sexual favours and overt comments of a sexual nature. However, there was insufficient evidence to prove any of the allegations against him and they were dropped. He never married because on a visit to Burma many years previously, he had been shot at by a deranged mountain farmer who took exception to an Englishman walking across his land. In Rangoon, the bullet which had lodged in his shoulder, was removed and on his return to England, it was kept in a ceramic vase on his mother's mantelpiece. Bentham sometimes complained of the wound in his shoulder but it seems that the damage was much lower, in a more intimate part of his body and that is why he never married. During his stay in KL, his old wound ceased to be troublesome and he began to feel virile pangs once more. He was at that time in his early 60s and it seemed too late in life for him to think about looking for a wife in the normal way. His good Malay friends persuaded him that it was never too late to seek romance and that he should visit Singapore, where many a Singapore girl had no aversion to marrying an older English gentleman, especially one 'in the money'.

And so, in due course, Bentham arrived in Singapore in search of his dream 'Singapore girl' who would be his future wife. He would, of course, explore that famous city and enjoy the sheer bliss of being pampered in Raffles Hotel where, hopefully, he might meet an oriental lady in search of an older man. She would have to be the slim and beautiful, Chinese but if she happened to be Indonesian or Filipina or Indian that would be fine. When it came to women, he was not in the least racist. The bane of his life was the puffed-up western woman.

He checked into the Raffles Hotel, that bastion of colonial pride and prestige. Where else would a man of his standing stay? He loved that hotel and the old colonial feel that it engenders. There, nobody would think it odd to find an elderly English gentleman clad in a brightly coloured batik shirt and khaki shorts having a Singapore Sling on the terrace of the hotel or sitting in the plush foyer, reading 'Crimson Sun Over Borneo'- that splendid novel by Prof. Hugh Hickling, the colonial lawyer who drafted the controversial Internal Security Act (ISA). As he turned the pages, he hoped that in his twilight years, he too might put pen to paper and write a memoir on his travels and work on behalf of the Commonwealth. His tale would reveal the other side of the legal profession and all its spicy deeds.

Bentham loved Singapore because he had long used it as a tax haven, safe from the probing eyes of UK Revenue. However, he was convinced that wealth was of little consolation without the joy of female companionship. Therefore, he was hoping that he might meet a charming Singapore girl who would be attracted by his good manners, elegance and wealth. His old friend at the Clarendon Club, Jonathan Goode, at the ripe old age of 65, had gone to Thailand and bought himself a charming wife. Maybe he too should do likewise.

Those were the thoughts swimming through his head when he suddenly looked up and saw an oriental goddess in a bright red dress enter the terrace and take a seat in an alcove by the window opposite his table, where she was instantly served a cold drink. She looked like a young executive type about to discuss a business deal with a prospective client as she opened her laptop and began tapping with long manicured fingers just like a classical pianist. Of course, Singapore is awash with beautiful oriental women – Chinese, Malay, Burmese and Filipina but the young lady in the red dress seemed especially endowed with grace and elegance. Bentham fumbled furiously in his mind for a pretext to attract her attention. He suddenly recalled the words of the English poet, Robert Herrick: 'Gather ye rosebuds while ye may'. Without more ado, he suddenly sprang up, walked straight over to her, and said: 'Excuse me, miss. Are you by any chance from Jardine & Chong in the city? I am expecting a visit from a member of that firm.' The lady shook her head and said that she was not that person. We do not know what else she said but we do know that she asked Bentham to take a seat and they engaged in conversation for over half an hour. It was all perfectly normal. There was nothing odd in two people having an extended conversation on the terrace of the Raffles Hotel. The drinks waiter confirmed that Bentham had ordered a Singapore sling for himself and a glass of champagne for the lady. At some point he went to the hotel shop and bought a red orchid which he presented to the lady. She seemed greatly pleased and placed it in her large Chanel handbag, which like her dress and shoes was red. She left the hotel around 5 p.m. and Bentham escorted her to the entrance where a taxi was waiting for her. He then returned to the terrace and ordered another Singapore sling. He looked very pleased and tipped the waiter generously. However, some time later he began to feel unwell and complained of a burning sensation in his abdomen and chest. He went to his room, lay on his bed and fell into a deep sleep. He never woke up.

Nobody knew what transpired during his meeting with the lady in red. It was assumed that somebody must have tampered with his Singapore sling. It was a sad ending for a noted English gentleman who was known and respected by the establishment in the UK and former colonies. It was obvious to me and to the Special Branch in Singapore that the 'dragon' – alias Amanda – must have been the lady in red who seduced Bentham with her charm and beauty. I was convinced that she had to be the killer. She matched our suspect's features – Chinese, very attractive, well-dressed, tall and slim and furthermore her victim in this case was a British subject of note, a man closely associated with the godfathers of colonialism. Once more, she had disappeared without a trace. The glasses in which the drinks were served had been washed and there was not a single piece of telltale evidence to identify her. The taxi driver was later located and he confirmed that he dropped her off in Orchard Road. We all assumed that she was the killer even though nobody could rule out the possibility that Bentham had died of natural causes, perhaps a heart attack or a deadly virus infection. At that time the SARS epidemic was raging across Southeast Asia and initially it was thought that he may have succumbed to the virus.

I had a meeting with the Director of Press Relations at the hotel but he could not shed much light on the matter. The only interesting piece of information that I manage to glean was that the CCTV system had been disabled that afternoon and consequently there was no footage of comings and goings. He did not seem to be aware of the fact that somebody must have disabled it. In fact, his main concern seemed to be to protect the good name of the Raffles Hotel. 'We must keep this mishap under wraps', he said. 'Sadly, some clients fall victim to the SARS virus.'

Naturally, Bentham's body was taken to the Singapore General Hospital where the noted toxicologist, Dr. Jacob Chan, conducted a post-mortem. I went to see him and as I sat there in the waiting area outside the Centre for Forensic Medicine my mind flashed back to Hitchcock's thriller 'Notorious' in which Claude Rains' evil mother kept sneaking poison drops into Ingrid Bergman's coffee.

Dr. Chan was most welcoming and he could obviously read my mind. 'Bad news, I'm afraid', he said. 'Poor Sir Rupert had a sad ending. Our toxicological analysis shows the deadly calomel, a mercurous chloride, which causes cardiac arrhythmia and, in many cases, instant death. I can confirm that he died of mercury poisoning. In plain English, he was terminated.'

Obviously, the visiting lady in the red dress had popped a deadly tablet in his drink while he was at the hotel shop. What I found most odd is the fact that not one of the hotel staff had any recollection of the event. Nobody had seen the young lady except the drinks waiter and he said she was no different from any other young Chinese lady. There must have been some insider collaboration since the CCTV system had been disabled. It was too much of a coincidence to believe that the system had gone down of its own accord while the 'dragon' was there. In Singapore, such things do not happen. The Singapore Special Branch would, of course, leave no stone unturned in seeking to solve the mystery. The problem is that most hotel workers in Singapore are migrants from the poorer parts of Southeast and their culture tells them to heed the maxim of the three wise monkeys: 'See no evil, hear no evil, speak no evil.' In New English that translates as: 'I not see nothing.'

A MAN ON A MISSION

In 2003, our Undersecretary for Defence Equipment and Arms Sales was Sir Robin Goddard OBE. My boss, Bonner-Davies, got to know him quite well. He was, like many in MI6 an old Oxfordian and 'a thoroughly decent chap', if I may use that phrase. He had been tireless in promoting Britain's arms industry overseas as a key component of the UK's economy. At that time, he was about to embark on a trade visit to Malaysia, Singapore and Brunei and he was very keen for MI6 to lobby for defence sales in our former colonies in Southeast Asia. He wanted our agents in the region to analyse the security threats and military needs of those wealthy client states and, where necessary, to bribe the relevant procurement chiefs. I could see the logic of his argument but I had mental reservations about the whole murky business of arm sales. Of course, I knew full well that ethical arguments were brushed aside whenever arms sales were debated in the House of Commons. I knew that Britain had a long history of arms sales, even to the world's most repressive regimes and would continue to do so more than ever in the future as we were about to leave the EU. We desperately needed to boost our overseas trade on all fronts. The oil-rich countries of the Middle East and Southeast Asia were eager to buy our military hardware, everything from assault rifles, machine guns, explosives, mines, teargas, munitions, grenade launchers to state-of-the-art defence systems, fighter aircraft, helicopter gunships, Chieftain tanks, missiles and nuclear submarines.

'Are you not defending the indefensible, Sir Robin', Bonner-Davies protested 'surely bribery and corruption should not be condoned. Why sell arms to such rogue states as Saudi Arabia, Burma and Sri Lanka? It's no wonder GB is accused of gross hypocrisy.'

'My good man, you know very well that if we do not provide our friends with military hardware, others will step in, in particular the Chinese and the Russians. Besides we need the cash and bribery has always played a key role in the sale of arms to our clients overseas.'

Sir Robin was confident that his trip to Kuala Lumpur would be a very profitable one. The Malaysian government had set aside billions of ringgit for upgrading its armed forces. The Ministry of Defence obviously needed more sophisticated weapons to counter the threat posed by the bellicose regime in North Korea and to a lesser extent the expansionist ambitions of Indonesia in Borneo. Both Singapore and Brunei were equally anxious to protect their borders by massive spending on military hardware and defence systems. Sir Robin had been fully briefed on those matters by the British High Commission and by Bonner-Davies, who had travelled to KL for that very purpose. The stage was set for the 'sale of the century'.

In KL where else would an old colonial stay except at the Shangri-la Hotel, a beautiful classic five-star hotel. There, Sir Robin was pampered not only by the hotel staff but by the High Commission which delegated one of its consular secretaries, Chandra Sastri, to see to his every need. On his second day in KL, Chandra arranged for Sir Robin to have dinner at the Outback Steakhouse - one of the best restaurants in Bukit Bintang. They dined off oysters, crispy fried mushrooms and the best Angus steak washed down with ice-cold Tiger beer. It was, as expected, a superb meal. Chandra was in his element. He was a fascinating conversationalist and he loved mixing with the upper class. 'I'm your minder,' to told Sir Robin. 'In KL one has to be street wise. Lots of bad eggs about, mostly from Nigeria and Indonesia.'

'Yes, one hears that everything bad is forbidden by law in KL but freely available, including flesh pots and opium dens,' whispered Sir Robin.

'Too true for you' responded Chandra, knowing full well that his protégé was partial to a little spicy recreational activity.

Few cities can match KL when it comes to the good life – la dolce vita. It has fabulous restaurants, night markets, bars and nightlife spots. Later that evening, Chandra took his guest to 'The Blue Lagoon' on Jalan Sultan, one of the many 'fun pubs' in the city. In KL, organized prostitution is outlawed but tolerated. Most of the working girls come from the Philippines, Indonesia, Thailand, Vietnam and China. Chandra ordered a large Scotch for Sir Robin and a pint of Guinness for himself. The drinks were served promptly by a very attractive girl in a red mini-dress so tight fitting that it seemed to have been put on with a spray gun. She had a slim body, raven black hair and a face that Helen of Troy would have envied. Naturally, Sir Robin fancied the exotic goddess.

'And how are you my pretty one?' he asked.

'I'm hunky-dory,' she replied.

Sir Robin winced at the Americanism but he was obviously enchanted by the goddess.

'Would you care to join us?' he asked.

'Sorry, I'm afraid we are rather busy right now. Perhaps later,' she replied and was gone.

Her English was fluent but her intonation was that of non-native speaker, quite choppy.

'She's probably an Indonesian chick or maybe a Chindian', ventured Chandra.

He explained that the word 'Chindian' was not in the Oxford Dictionary but in Southeast Asia it is freely used to denote a person of mixed race, part Chinese and part Indian.

'A deadly combination,' he said. He went on to voice his views on beautiful women. He lowered his voice and whispered to Sir Robin: 'When it comes to oriental women, be very careful. They appear as dazzling butterflies but beneath that alluring exterior, the lady may be a cunning vixen, a vampire, a dragon or even a 'hantu' (a spirit). You may not believe it but here in Southeast Asia witchcraft and black magic are common. Most of all, beware the dreaded Pontianak - the blood-sucking vampire that preys on men of means. She lures them into the jungle where they disappear forever.'

'Don't worry. I shall watch my back,' said Sir Robin in obvious jest. He finished his drink and lit up a cigar. He liked the relaxed ambiance of 'The Blue Lagoon', the charming clientele and the lively dance music played by a Filipino trio.

'One for the road?' suggested Chandra.

'Why not indeed!' replied Sir Robin.

The drinks were served by a very gay-looking young man who moved with the grace of a ballet dancer. Sir Robin said: 'Wow! Now that's what I call a real Bloody Mary' as he tipped the waiter. The young man bowed graciously and said: 'Avec plaisir.' However, when he was out of earshot, Sir Robin said: 'I was rather hoping the girl in the red mini dress would have served the drinks.'

As the two men sipped their drinks, they chatted freely about a certain British MP who was seen out of trousers in a seedy KL fun pub. 'We all do silly things when we drink too much,' said Chandra. The bar was packed and everyone was having a great time. However, Chandra noticed that Sir Robin had begun twitching in his seat and wiping his brow with a handkerchief. His Billy Bunter face seemed to go a darker shade of red and his eyes began watering. At first, Chandra put it down to the absence of fresh air in a bar clouded in cigarette and cigar smoke. A few minutes later Sir Basil said that he felt unwell and dashed to the WC. Chandra was a worried man. He suspected it might be a case of 'tummy rot' most likely caused by the oysters they had for dinner. Sir Robin was scheduled to attend a passing out parade of cadets at the Royal Military College the following morning. The RMC is near the township of Sungai Besi, a few miles outside KL. There, he would meet and build a good working relationship with the top brass of the armed forces of Malaysia, Singapore and Brunei.

Since his protégé had not returned, Chandra dashed to the WC. He found Sir Robin slumped over a wash-hand basin, his whole body trembling in a paroxysm of pain. He complained of a tingling sensation in his hands and feet. His skin seemed to have darkened. Clearly, he was in a bad way. He had difficulty in breathing and was experiencing violent cramps and a feeling of nausea. Chandra asked a member of staff to escort Sir Basil to a rest room while he reported the matter to the manager. The manager, fearing the worst, immediately called an ambulance and had Sir Basil rushed to the Emergency Department of the Assunta Hospital. However, it was to no avail. He lapsed into a coma and on arrival at the hospital he was pronounce dead.

Chandra immediately called me saying: 'Meet me at 'The Blue Lagoon' right away. I shall inform the police chief to get here as soon as possible in order to gather whatever forensic evidence is available.' However, on arrival, the police chief found no forensic evidence whatever. The drinks glasses had been collected and washed and the lady in the red mini-dress had vanished. Nobody in the pub had noticed anything suspicious. In KL a lot of very sexy girls can be seen in fun pubs. They come and go in search of business. The manager informed the police chief, Det. Inspector Yakob and me that all the serving girls wore green uniforms supplied by the club. Neither he nor his staff had noticed the lady in the red mini-dress. Chandra insisted that somebody must have noticed her but his comment was met with a wall of silence.

We then rushed to the hospital in Petaling Jaya where we met Dr. Moses Bhatia, a specialist in toxicology. He confirmed that Sir Robin was dead on arrival. Furthermore, he confirmed that he had died within 30 minutes of consuming a lethal dose of arsenic.

'Have you ruled out food poisoning?' Chandra asked. 'He had had oysters for dinner.'

'Well, we know it was not food poisoning. No. He died of arsenic poisoning. Of that, there is no doubt. What we do not know is whether it was caused by accidental ingestion or intentional poisoning, - in other words, murder.'

'Oh my God!' cried Chandra, 'Are you sure? I have heard that arsenic poisoning is not unknown in remote areas where people consume contaminated groundwater.'

'That is so,' responded Dr. Moses 'but in urban centres it is hardly ever found in water or food. My view is that in this case somebody deliberately laced the victim's drink with arsenic. Even a tiny amount of inorganic arsenic is fatal to humans. Furthermore, I can confirm that the amount ingested by the deceased could have killed an elephant.'

'In that case, we shall want a full forensic post-mortem? Can that be done forthwith?' asked Chandra.

'That will not be necessary' said Dr. Moses. 'We now have a simple method of detecting poisonous substances in the human body. Hair-follicle analysis will confirm whether arsenic is present. We are already running the test. The finding will be known within the hour. Please wait in the cafeteria upstairs. I am not allowed to hand out the complete report but I can let you see the summary.

About 30 minutes later, we received the summary, which is reproduced here.

Name of subject: Robin Goddard OBE
Date: 12.9.2003
Time of death: 10.20 p.m.
Details of subject: British subject, age 49.
Next of kin: cf. British High Commission, KL.
Test: Hair-follicle analysis
Clinic: Lab 4.1
Operator: Valerie Chin
Cause of death: Cardiac arrest due to arsenic poising
Type of poison: Arsenic trioxide
Strength of dosage: LD50(30 mg/kg)

'Damn, damn, damn!' were the only words Chandra could utter. He had reason to be deeply upset. After all, he was supposed to be minding Sir Robert. The killing of an eminent British MP in KL could not be swept under the carpet. The High Commission would have to release a statement expressing regret over his demise and also confirm that the Malaysian authorities were investigating the circumstances surrounding it. We knew that once his body was returned to the UK, the High Commission and MI6 would get a bashing from the hostile British media. However, there was no way the KL police or MI6 could admit that a prominent British MP had been murdered and that his assassin was still at large. Fortunately, Datuk Kassim Ahmed, a spokesman for the Ministry of Information in KL, came up with a creative solution. His plan was to create a press release which stated that

Sir Robin had died in circumstances which were unclear. It went on to state that within hours of his death, the KL Special Branch, acting on tip-off from a taxi-driver, had arrested a suspect. Her name could not as yet be released for legal reasons but it was stated that she was most probably an Indonesian female, working as a prostitute in the city. She confessed that she had placed a pinch of a white powder in Sir Robin's drink. She did not know that it was poison. She thought that it was syabu, which is freely available from drug dealers all over KL. Her intention was to sedate him and then come back and pick his pocket.

Next day, a further press release would state that the suspect was being held in a high security prison in the city and that she would be tried in the Criminal Court later that month. The expectation was that she would be sentenced to death for her crime, unless the presiding judge decided that there were mitigating circumstances, in which case she might be deported to her homeland. I should add that I had no part to play in the cover-up story because in MI6 we either say nothing about such matters or tell the truth.

The modern habit of using 'fake news' in order to influence public opinion most probably originated in Southeast Asia. Governments there are very good at it. I was shocked to hear of the monstrous plan dreamed up by the Ministry of Information and Bonner-Davies too had indicated his displeasure, but Datuk Kassim insisted that 'fake news' was better than no news. If his office was to admit to the world that the Sir Robin's killer was still at large, that she had already killed three other British high-profile victims and that nobody had the faintest clue as to her identity, location or identity, the Malaysian police and government would be accused of gross incompetence and questions might be asked about the affair in the House of Commons. Moreover, MI6 would certainly get it in the neck from the hostile press in the UK. Furthermore, Bonner-Davies had a very angry call from the Foreign Secretary in Whitehall. He was not impressed with our performance and, in the most unparliamentary language imaginable, he said that he expected MI6 to stop pussyfooting and catch the killer of his esteemed fellow MP forthwith or heads would roll. He did not seem to realize that the Malaysian Special Branch, the Singaporean Special Branch and MI6 were working round the clock to track the killer down.

The response to Datuk Kassim's 'fake news' press release was greeted with derision and disbelief in London. 'The Daily Dispatch' called it a 'ha ha' story, which it undoubtedly was. Bonner-Davies was repeatedly vilified in the media. His detractors stated openly that MI6 was a bunch of incompetents who could not find an elephant in a china shop. That kind of disrespect is very hurtful to those of us working overseas, risking our lives daily in the national interest.

What worried me and Bonner-Davies even more was that the suspect – the lady in red – seemed to be a serial killer and that she was still at large. What would she do next? Would she strike again and if so, where? Was she acting alone or with the backing of a foreign power, for instance the People's Republic? Could she be a Chinese secret agent, under instructions from Beijing to extinguish British influence and disrupt arms sales in Southeast Asia? Bonner-Davies and I urgently needed to find answers to these and many other questions. Clearly, the killer was highly intelligent and well informed about the location and activity of her victims. For instance, in the case of Sir Robin, she knew he was staying at the Shangri-la Hotel. She must have known that he and Chandra had dined at the 'Outback Steakhouse' and later that evening that they had gone to 'The Blue Lagoon'. She must have known about murder by poison – a method as old as Socrates. She obviously knew that arsenic is the most effective poison for killing a person; it is safer than other poisons in that it is both untraceable and fast-acting. Where did she acquire the considerable knowledge to know how to prepare and administer deadly chemical agents. It was tempting to assume that she had a degree in chemistry. What was equally alarming was her ability to operate unseen. One thing was clear. The killer was more than a pretty face. Perhaps Chandra was right. He suggested that she might be a professional killer, working in conjunction with an underground organization or that she might even be an Indonesian Pontianak, a blood-sucking vampire who resides inside the trunk of ancient trees and often appears in bars and night clubs in order to attract male victims. Whatever about a roaming vampire, it seemed to me that our suspect had bizarre knowledge and power. I had no idea how we were going to catch her. She appeared to be invisible and continued to evade us with all the cunning of a dragon.

THE NET CLOSES

In September 2003 everyone across Southeast Asia was living in fear of the dragon, not knowing where or when she might strike next. My boss, Bonner-Davis, was worried at our lack of progress in tracking her down. The mysterious killer was now widely referred to as 'the dragon'. Of course, MI6 works in close cooperation with the CIA and the Secret Service in Malaysia and Singapore. We had over the years greatly assisted the Malaysian Special Branch (SB) on many successful counterterrorism operations. At that time the SB Director of Operation was Datuk Abdul Razak bin Sharif. I had met him a few times previously and found him to be well informed and highly regarded by all of us in the security services. He was in charge of a large army of agents worldwide, all tasked with combating terrorists and criminals who threatened the national security while also protecting the lives of high-profile people, both domestic and foreign. However, in the media, he was regarded as a 'hard man', hard on crime and especially hard on terrorism.

Like every other secret service organization, the Malaysian Special Branch (SB) is involved in surveillance and intelligence gathering. However, every taxi drive will tell you that the Malaysian SB is really a 'deep state' – a state withing the state, used by the BN coalition to silence, abduct and detain 'enemies of the state'. It was said to be deeply involved in infiltrating and spying on opposition parties, pro-democracy activists, Chinese and Indian radicals, leftist academics, bloggers and critics of the government. Hence, its real purpose seemed to be to generate a culture of fear and intimidation. Much had been revealed in the media about its covert operations and its involvement in cracking down on dissidents and subversives, its interrogation and torture methods, its embezzlement of government funds, its role in the Anwar Ibrahim sodomy scandal and the disappearance of certain high-profile critics of the government. Naturally, I did not discuss any of those matters with Abdul Razak. Instead, we talked about football, Formula 1 racing and current affairs.

At that time the Malaysian Special Branch was deeply involved in the surveillance of Islamic terrorists - members of al-Qaeda and trusted followers of Osama bin Laden. It was well known that those bearded gentlemen were more than political activists; they were hard-core terrorists, hell bent on getting their hands on biological and chemical weapons, planning bank robberies, kidnappings, suicide bombings and assassinations. For reasons I cannot explain, I wondered whether the 'dragon' we were both chasing might target Abdul Razak. She would have known about his role in harassing Chinese, Indian and Malay intellectuals, writers and political activists who constantly denounced the misrule and corruption of the Federal government. It was widely assumed that it was he who fabricated all manner of fake scandals about opposition members of parliament in order to have them changed with moral depravity and sent to a detention centre or prison.

I knew that Abdul Razak was aware of the activities of the so-called dragon and her campaign of killing. Every agent and police officer in the country was doing their utmost to hunt her down but with no success whatever. After each killing episode, the dragon disappeared like a ghost in the forest. Our man in KL kept Abdul Razak informed of her crimes but of course none of us knew what her next move might be nor who might be her next victim. All we knew was that she seemed to target high-profile persons. MI6 worked hand in hand with the Malaysian SB but of course we did not approve of Abdul Razak's manner of dealing with the people he called subversives, dissidents and communists. My boss held him in high esteem and it was he who invited Abdul Razak to the conference on terrorism which MI5, MI6 and the Metropolitan Police had planned for London in November that year. In fact, Abdul Razak was asked to address the conference as a keynote speaker.

On 5th November 2003 I had arranged to meet Abdul Razak at KL Airport. I was asked to help him prepare his presentation and to inform him that it should focus more on the motivation of terrorists rather than on their campaign of terror. 'Not to worry, old chap' he said, 'I know the mind of the terrorist better than anyone.' On the flight to London, I was glad of the opportunity to review with him each of the killings carried out by 'the dragon' and to piece together the fragments of evidence we had managed to collect on her case. We were hoping that the conference might shed some light on the motivation of our killer and possible suggest a better way to track her down. On arrival at Heathrow, a police car was waiting to take Abdul Razak directly to the Dorchester Hotel. I promised to see him the following day and possibly have dinner with him in one of the Malaysian restaurants nearby.

What neither Abdul Razak nor I realized was that on the same flight there was a young Chinese lady seated at the rear of the economy class. Later that day Immigration contacted my boss in MI6 to advice that young Chinse lady named Estelle Fu-Cheng had arrived and that she bore some resemblance to the young Malaysian lady known as 'the dragon' on the wanted list. The young lady told Immigration that she was planning to attend an Open Day at Westminster University with a view to enrolling on their MBA degree course commencing in January 2004. She said that she was staying at the Strand Palace Hotel. Immigration then called the hotel which confirmed that it had a booking in that name. My boss, Bonner-Davies, notified Flanagan and MI5 of the danger and I was instructed to proceed to the Dorchester Hotel the following day in order to advise Abdul Razak to be on his guard in case he had an unexpected visit from Ms. Fu-Cheng. It was all mere speculation, of course. At any hint of trouble, MI5 and MI6 always assume the worst and take whatever action seems necessary.

The next day, Chief Superintendent Flanagan and I made our way to the Dorchester to make sure that Abdul Razak was aware of our concern for his safety. Being a VIP, he had booked a large penthouse suite. Few hotels can match the elegance of the Dorchester and its famous Harlequin Suite which was described by Alfred Hitchcock as the perfect place to commit a murder, presumably because it overlooks Hyde Park, where a body could be easily buried. I was not in the least apprehensive of such a dire event. In fact, I was looking forward to having tea on the terrace and a chat about the latest gossip coming out of KL. In Malaysia, every café is always alive with gossip about the latest political scandal, which more often than not has no basis in truth. In Malay culture, it is perfectly normal to add spicy details to every story that appears in the media.

We arrived at the Dorchester Hotel shortly after 4 p.m. Abdul Razak assumed that we were on a courtesy visit. He was visibly shaken when I informed him about the young Chinese lady who was on our flight to London the previous day and had booked into the Stand Palace Hotel.

Flanagan added: 'We may be on to something here. Immigration advised us check her out. It may well be a wild goose chase since even if the young lady was the dreaded dragon, she could not possibly know that you are in London or that you are was staying in the Dorchester Hotel.'

'My God!' blurted Abdul Razak. 'She may have discovered that I am attending the conference. Our HQ leaks like a sieve and the KL media announced that the Special Branch would be represented at the conference by a senior officer. It would not take her long to figure out that I was that person. Of course, we may be reading too much into the situation but given her record of targeted killings, I might well be her next target.'

'Indeed', agreed Flanagan, 'in that case you'd better remain here in case the dragon is up to mischief. We shall keep her under observation and we will have an officer on watch in the hotel foyer. It may all be a damp squib but you never know with dragons!'

Abdul Razak seemed reassured by that remark and he invited us to join him for tea on the terrace. It was not just tea and scones. It was high tea in the best colonial tradition – in other words a feast designed for refined palates.

THE ENDGAME

As we sat on the terrace of the Dorchester Hotel enjoying a sumptuous high tea, little did we know that the young lady we suspected of being 'the dragon' had already left her hotel and gone go Chinatown. There, in Cope Lane, she made her way to a seedy shophouse called Kwee-Shen's which sells a variety of tobaccos, clove cigarettes and vaping devices. Mr. Kwee does a brisk trade in e-liquids with fancy names such as Vape Juice, Oriental e-liquid, Herbal Mist, etc. all of which are perfectly legal in the UK. However, Kwee-Shen's is also a dope-shop, offering a wide selection of illegal drugs – cannabis, ecstasy, cocaine, heroin, LSD, amphetamines and opium. In addition, to select customers only, Mr. Kwee also sells a concoction called Dragon Vape, which is a highly toxic liquid. Naturally, all transactions are kept secret since he knows how to deal with informers. He does not look like a drugs baron. He is small of stature, quite bald like a Buddhist monk, clean shaven, dressed in a loose orange smock and black trousers. The young lady approached the counter and said: 'May I speak with Mr. Kwee. I have urgent business.' The man replied: 'I Kwee. I very busy. No time to talk with stranger.' The young lady insisted. 'Please don't mess with me. I need a vial of Dragon Vape.' Mr. Kwee had no idea who she was and he waved her away, saying: 'No smokey juice. No hab stock.' However, when she thrust a wad of ten-pound notes into his hand, he paused, and said: 'Ok, just one item, la.' Then he went behind the partition and soon returned with a vial of Dragon Vape which he handed over with a verbal health warning: 'Missie, no inhale any. Very toxic.' In a flash, the young lady was gone.

On her way back to the hotel she stopped at a corner shop and bought a packet of King Edward cigars. Then stopping at Boots, she bought a hypodermic syringe. Back in the hotel, she opened the packet of cigars and injected each with 0.25ml of Dragon Vape. Then she sealed the packet and placed it in her handbag. Obviously, the cigars were intended for a person with a fondness for the King Edward brand. When injected with the liquid, the cigars become a deadly weapon.

At 5 p.m. the young lady took a cab to the Dorchester Hotel. She was dressed in a discreet blue uniform with a badge saying 'Elite Escort Services'. On arrival at the hotel she went to reception, saying that she was Ami Tan from 'Elite Escort Services'. She wished to see a Malaysian client, Mr. Abdul Razak bin Sharif, to help him make the most of his visit to London. The lady in reception was satisfied with the young lady's bona fides and directed her to the Harlequin Suite.

Flanagan and I were about to leave when the doorbell rang. We stayed out of sight behind the sliding door to the terrace. Then Abdul Razak peered through the peephole and rubbed his eyes in disbelief. Before him stood an elegant young lady in a blue uniform. As he opened the door, the visitor greeted him warmly saying she was Ami Tan on a routine visit to the hotel to see if clients needed any help with booking events, tours, shows, etc. She said: 'We take all the pain out of having fun. Our service includes a substantial discount on entry fees to shows and events, taxi fares, dining, etc. Just call the agency if you are interested.' Abdul Razak was reassured by her smart appearance and her business-like manner. Clearly, he was more interested in the young lady than the services she offered. He knew that Flanagan and I were eavesdropping on the terrace, noting her every word, ready to pounce at any moment. He asked the lady to take a seat while he checked his diary. Flanagan and I listened carefully from behind the sliding door to the terrace. Even though the lady spoke English fluently she did so with the intonation typical of Chinese speakers. I noticed that her pronunciation of certain vowel and consonant clusters was typical of Malaysian speakers. Abdul Razak sat down behind his oak desk and began: 'I'm afraid I won't have very much free time. I have a very busy week ahead.' As soon as he said that the young lady stood up and said: 'Well, it's up to you sir. Just call our agency if you need a booking or guided tour.' As she prepared to depart, she handed him a small gift-wrapped item, saying: 'We always give our clients a small gift.' He removed the wrapping and held up a packet of King Edward cigars.

'Splendid! I hardly deserve this,' he said. 'You have good taste.' However, one could see a question mark on his face. How did the lady know that he had a fondness for King Edward cigars? At that point, Flanagan and I emerged from the terrace.

At long last we had come face to face with the dragon. I rubbed my eyes in disbelief. Our mock-up photofit of the dragon was quite wide of the mark. The young lady before us was tall and slim with a body that Lara Croft would have envied. She was a carbon copy of the oriental models that are often featured on the cover page of Vogue. In simple terms, she was a beautiful woman. For me the beauty of a woman is not in the figure she carries or the clothes she wears; it is her face that defies her beauty and her personality. In MI6 we are good at reading faces. We do it every day. I can tell an honest face at a glance just as I can tell a devious one. Facial features do not lie. The lady's face was pure gold; it radiated charm and elegance. I found it hard to believe that we were looking into the face of a killer.

'I should like to try one of your cigars', Flanagan said to the young lady who suddenly froze like a statue. She must have known then that the game was up. She glanced about like a cornered animal. 'Am I being arrested, and if so, on what grounds?' she asked.

'Let's say you are being detained by the Special Branch for questioning. It seems that we have quite a lot to talk about. Not now of course, but in the morning.'

Det. Inspector Flanagan had no difficulty in deciding to hold the suspect in police custody, pending a formal charge. It would be up to the Crown Prosecution Service (CPU) to charge her with attempted homicide. The arresting officer must provide sufficient evidence for the

CPU to warrant the issue of a 'charge sheet' setting out the details of the crime that the suspect was being charged with. Prior to that moment, all we had was circumstantial evidence. We had good reason to suspect that our suspect was the killer we were chasing for months across Southeast Asia. We assumed that she was responsible for the killing of six British subjects there and that she had come to London to terminate one more victim, namely the head of the Malaysian Special Branch.

I was utterly baffled. The Malaysian Special Branch has agents everywhere and, just like MI6, it has online surveillance systems gathering data on wanted persons every hour of the day. I can check on the location and movement of a named person on my monitor at any time. Yet neither the Special Branch not MI6 could get a fix on the young lady we now knew as 'the dragon'. How did she manage to carry out her targeted killings for a whole year across Southeast Asia without leaving a trace. We had a few possible leads of no great significance. Now, we had absolute proof of her murderous intention. But for our intervention, we were quite sure that she would have killed Abdul Razak bin Sharif. Her cover about being an escort girl was blown. We contacted the Elite Escort agency and were informed that no such person was employed by them. Then we contacted the forensic lab requesting a test of the suspect's body samples and all her belongings. We were told that a full forensic process would take a day or two depending on the number and type of samples collected and submitted. However, the toxicology analyst indicated that he could test the cigars right away and let us have the result later that evening. We already had one vital piece of information, her real name. In her handbag, we found her passport and airline ticket, both of which were in the name of Estelle Fu-Cheng and her home address was stated as Kuching, Sarawak. She may have been a dragon but she was now in captivity. She did not spend the night in the Strand Palace Hotel; she spent it in the Victoria Embankment police prison.

My boss, Bonner-Davies was very pleased that we had at last apprehended the dragon. He read my report on the matter of her capture with a certain wry amusement. I think perhaps he liked my gushing style of writing. He called me into his office and chuckled as he read my description of the dragon. It says: 'She has a flawless olive complexion and that inscrutable oriental look that seems to say: How dare you lesser mortals gaze upon a goddess! Her sloe-black eyes look like black sapphires chiselled out of marble. Her raven black hair is neatly plaited in a ponytail and...' At that point he suddenly paused me and said: 'My good man, this is too rich! Are you a scriptwriter or what? We shall have to suppress the poet in you.' With that, he reached for the bottle of Chivas Regal and two tumblers that he keeps the on topmost shelf of his bookshelf. He poured a generous glass of the liquid into each tumbler and said: 'Down the hatch, old boy! May we all live every day of our life, safe from marauding dragons.'

THE CONFESSION

The next morning Estelle was interrogated by Detective Inspector Flanagan over a two-hour period while our recorder, Miss Doran and I listened and took note of key points. She spoke swiftly with good humour, showing no rancour whatever. She seemed totally unconcerned by the predicament in which she now found herself. It seemed that she was resigned to her fate. The session was video recorded and transcribed. The typescript runs to 60 pages, much too long to reproduce here. Hence, it will suffice to mention the main points which emerged.

She said that her name was Estelle Fu-Cheng. She told us that her great, great, grandfather was Pastor Wong Nai Siong who was responsible for bringing over a thousand Foochow Chinese to Sibu in 1901. He did so with the approval of the second White Rajah. The Rev. Wong was a devout Methodist and it was he who built the first school and hospital in Sibu. His grandson, Ruben Huang, became a prominent member of the Borneo Communist Party. He was charged with sedition, imprisoned and died in prison in 1960. Estelle vowed never to forgive the Chief Minister and his British backers for Huang's death; not only that but also for branding her people 'the yellow peril' and treating them as second-class citizens. She vowed then to exact retribution. She would do it in her own way and in her own time. 'One has to fight fire with fire', she said.

We had already received the toxicology report on the King Edward cigars. It stated that each cigar contained a deadly mix of morphine, heroin and opium. It added that when the liquid is heated it creates a toxic vapour which if inhaled by the user would be fatal. A puff of the toxic substance was sufficient to trigger an explosion, shattering a person's jaw and if inhaled, causing instant death. The name Dragon Vape was apt since real dragons kill their prey with a single bite and the victim dies from the toxins in the dragon's saliva. The report was damning evidence of Estelle's murderous intent. Her visit to the Dorchester Hotel had been a massive blunder; she had been hoisted with her own petard. All that we needed was a confession by her. However, we had no idea whether she would try to wriggle out of her unfortunate situation.

'We shall talk about your motivation presently but first tells us why you have come to London?' asked Flanagan.

'You know very well why I came here. I came here on behalf of my people in order to terminate a very evil man, namely Abdul Razak bin Sharif, Commander of the Malaysian Special Branch.'

Flanagan replied: 'Hold on! No law-abiding citizen has the right to terminate a person's life. In what sense is Abdul Razak an evil man? Can you tell us why you acted as you did? Were you driven by malice, or ideology or something else?'

Estelle said: 'My parents were very religious and they used to say that I was driven by 'bad seed'. They may be right. I seem to have a black voice in the back of my head that colours my thinking, my emotions and my moods. However, that voice seems to be the voice of the oppressed during the dark days of colonialism, reflecting the collective consciousness of Chinese people across Southeast Asia. We have been suppressed for too long and the suppression of Chinese culture, values and identity continues under our so-called 'independent' Federation.

Flanagan said: 'I can understand the legacy issues which, as you say, still persist in Malaysia. But why target an innocent man like Datuk Abdul Razak?'

Estelle then listed several instances of criminal activity conducted by the Malaysian SB under instructions from Abdul Razak and with the approval of the government. According to Estelle, those 'evil deeds' were the following:

In 1997, the noted history professor and author of 'The History of Southeast Asia', Dr. Ronald Goh, had challenged the government over its revised history syllabus and textbooks for secondary schools. He objected to the inclusion of new elements on patriotism, citizenship and the constitution. He claimed that the teaching of history was being distorted by an ethno-nationalist approach which asserted that Malaysia was an Islamic state and that only Malays were 'Bumiputera' (sons of the soil). All other people were 'foreign races' and as such were untrustworthy and entitled to fewer rights and privileges. It was not long before Dr. Goh was subjected to systemic denigration and harassment. He knew that eventually he would be changed with sedition under the recently revised Sedition Act. He did not wait to be sent to the Taiping Detention Centre in Perak and he wisely fled to New Zealand. Estelle added: 'You see, dissidents are not tolerated in Malaysia. They are either in jail or in exile.'

Estelle said that she could give several more instances of trumped-up charges against Chinese and Indian writers, academics and trade union leaders who were detained and brutally treated in Malaysia's Gulag, i.e., the Taiping Detention Centre in Perak. One such person was a journalist and blogger in Shah Alam called Samy Mohan. At first, he had criticised the ruling party's race-based policies and endemic corruption but later his barbs became more pointed and personal. He accused the Special Branch and its Commander, Abdul Razak of embezzlement and police brutality. He said that they were 'nothing more than thieves' and that Malaysian was fast becoming a police state. Abdul Razak was not amused. He had Samy arrested and brutally beaten at the police station in Shah Alam. He was blindfolded, stripped naked, cold water was poured over him, his mouth was forced open and he was forced to drink urine. After several weeks of torture, the police authorities there announced that Samy Mohan had committed suicide. It was said that he had jumped to his death from the 4th floor of H-block onto the concrete concourse. His body was not released for burial and no post-mortem took place. Everyone suspected foul play but had no evidence until several weeks later when another prisoner, Danny Loo, managed to escape in a laundry van. It was he who revealed what really happened. He told the press that political prisoners were held in solitary confinement in a tiny cell, with no window but only air vents in the wall. They slept on a foam mattress on the floor and their toilet was a hole in the floor. He knew that Samy bad been mercilessly tortured on orders from Abdul Razak who actually came to the prison on one occasion and punched him black and blue. A few days later, Danny Loo was assigned to laundry duty. On his rounds he heard a commotion on the 4th floor. He dashed up and saw Samy being dragged along the corridor and being lashed by two prison guards. He noticed that the barred window at the end of the corridor had been opened wide. He saw Samy being pushed through the open window to his death below. Eventually, Amnesty International took up the case which became known as 'the defenestration of Shah Alam.'

Turning to me, Estelle said: 'You must be familiar with that case which was widely reported in the 'Straits Times' and the 'Borneo Gazette'. Then she added 'You must also be quite familiar with the great embezzlement scandal known as 'The RM 10.5 billion scandal'. I said that I had read a report claiming that 80% of Malaysian law enforcement and security officers were corrupt but I had no knowledge of the Multi-billion Scandal. Flanagan then asked Estelle to explain how it related Abdul Razak. She did so with great ease and aplomb.

Prior to the 1999 General Election, the political climate in Sabah and Sarawak was of particular interest to the Federal government due to sensitivities about secession from the Federation. There was widespread discontent over the failure of the government to implement the terms of the 'Malaysia Agreement 1963' which guaranteed to the new members the same rights and entitlements as the other Malayan states and Singapore. The agreement included the right to secede from the Federation if the agreement was not honoured. Accordingly, on advice from the Special Branch, the government set aside a RM 10.5 billion fund for a range of infrastructure projects in Sarawak, especially schools and clinics for the indigenous people. However, not one of those projects was delivered and the money disappeared into deep pockets.

The main beneficiary of the rip-off was the Malaysian Special Branch under its corrupt chief, Abdul Razak bin Sharif.

Estelle went on: 'Today, Abdul Razak bin Sharif is one of the richest men in Malaysia and, ironically, his Special Branch is charged with uncovering the mastermind behind the embezzlement. He should look in the mirror. Naturally, nobody has so far been apprehended. It was put out that certain Chinese and Indian civil servants had stolen the money and absconded. However, every dog on the street knows what happened. We all know who stole the money. Malaysia is now one of the most corrupt states in the world.'

Pointing her finger directly at Flanagan, she said: 'You should be ashamed. The UK is colluding with a regime involved in torture and extrajudicial executions.' On that point, Flanagan assured her the British security services did not execute anyone; they put suspected criminals and terrorists away and they shared intelligence with friends in Southeast Asia in order to counter terrorism. He said: 'We would never condone the brutal suppression of pro-democracy activists not a corruption-ridden police force. I do not understand what you are about. Are you a rebel, or a subversive or a terrorist?

Estelle smiled and said: 'Those are all loaded terms used by the ruling regime to silence those of us who defend democracy and human rights. If you want to change an entrenched political system which is racist, self-serving and utterly corrupt, you have to sling a few bombs around. The problem is the lack of democracy. My protest is against abuse of power by the ruling elite in Putrajaya, in each of the Malay States, in Singapore and Brunei. Democracy simply does not exist in Southeast Asia.'

Flanagan did not point an accusing finger at Estelle, nor raise his voice like an angry schoolmaster. He showed a degree of understanding almost as if he wished to overlook her offences. At the same time, he failed to understand what was gained by killing people who were for some reason deemed expendable.

'Surely if you intentionally kill people because you disagree with their ideology, you are a terrorist,' suggested Flanagan.

'And who created the terrorists in the first place?' replied Estelle. 'I suggest that it was your government's colonial policies in the past and, right now, the ugly nationalism of the BN party in Putrajaya, the feudal regime in Brunei and the authoritarian PAP party in Singapore.' It was obvious that Estelle had no compunction over the mission on which she had embarked. For her it was a moral crusade, a sort of biblical retribution, 'an eye for an eye'. She had to scatter the evil ones like chaff.

Flanagan then informed Estelle that he was charging her with conspiracy to commit murder and that she would be remanded in custody at the Victoria Detention Centre pending her trial in the Special Criminal Court several weeks later. He also pointed out that in the UK a charge of attempted murder carries a mandatory 40-year mandatory sentence. Nowadays, however, because prisons are overflowing, prison governors are only too happy to reduce a long sentence to five or ten years if they were confident that the prisoner will not re-offend and if the Home Secretary has no objection. Eventually, one's fate is sealed by the judge, who, on the day, might be lenient or draconian. Some UK judges are tough on crime, especially when they see a foreign person standing before them in the dock. He added that her prison cell would be spartan and austere, all sparkling clean, smelling of Dettol. She would have good food, reading material, a radio and television. She could have counselling and free legal advice. However, she would not be allowed visits or communication with the outside world.

Estelle covered her face in her hands and looked visibly shaken by this unexpected turn of events. She knew that the game was up. She remained silent for several minutes, before saying in response: 'Well, in that case, I would like to make a statement, in fact a confession. I am guilty on the count you have named and I hope the court will understand why I acted as I did. But what happens if the court decides to deport me to Malaysia?' On that point, Flanagan said: 'Malaysia may request that you be deported once you have served your time here. Crimes committed overseas are subject to the that jurisdiction. However, we do not deport people to a country known to have a flawed judicial system.'

Finally, Flanagan drafted a statement which was signed by Estelle, confessing that (i) she had come to London to terminate the Commander of the Malaysian Special Branch, Abdul Razak bin Sharif, and (ii) prior to her visit to London, she was responsible for the killing of five British subjects in Sarawak, Sabah, Labuan and Kuala Lumpur. Moreover, (iii) she had acted alone and was not part of any terrorist organization and (iv) that she had acted out of moral concern for the defence of democracy and human rights across Southeast Asia.

The confession was witnessed and filed by Miss Doran at the police station.

14

THE SHADOW

'It is a frightening thought that man
also has a shadow side to him,
consisting not just of little weaknesses
and foibles, but a positively
demonic dynamism.' (Carl Jung)

Bonner-Davies and I were very pleased to have captured the dragon
before attending the conference on 'The Mind of the Terrorist' which
was convened by the Minister for Home Affairs in order to advise
the government on drafting new legislation to deal with the rise of
terrorism and radicalisation. The recent arrest of 'the dragon' was a
major topic of conversation and I was commended for my part in that
operation. Even grumpy old Mr. Naylor patted me on the back and
said: 'Glad you chaps in MI6 have at last managed to achieve something
worthwhile.'

Those of us who work in national security services are baffled by the
fact that certain individuals commit horrendous crimes and very often
defy all attempts to track them down. For the best part of a year, I had
been led a merry chase across Southeast Asia by a young Chinese lady
who was labelled a serial killer by the police in Malaysia and Singapore

but to me she seemed more aptly described as a misguided idealist. Apart from the fact that she had a fondness for wearing a red dress decorated with dragon motifs, she seemed to possess the attributes of the scheming dragon. And of course, we know that in Chinese culture the dragon is king – the symbol of power, wisdom and goodness or evil.

Professor Zac Hammond, the noted American criminologist, happened to be one of the keynote speakers at a conference on 'The Mind of the Terrorist'. Most of the presentations and workshops dealt with the rise of Islamic terrorism, radicalisation and post-colonial legacy issues. In the British model of terrorist detection, the focus was on containment. The strategies and techniques of the terrorist were studied and procedures for detecting and apprehending those engaged in terrorism were developed and tested. However, according to Professor Hammond, the US model of dealing with terrorism was more robust but it was not working. The focus there was on physical force and armed response more than on going upstream to uncover the social, cultural or historical underpinnings of terrorism. Terrorism was like a deadly virus that spread like wildfire unless the source was located and dealt with. One had to look beyond the situation and not jump to conclusions too soon. One had to tune in to the local culture and take soundings from the community. 'Listen to the sound of the river and you will be able to catch the fish,' he said. He did not think that the 'shoot first' policy in the US was an effective strategy. He said: 'There is always a reason why things happen.' He also pointed out that British people had a poor understanding of the cultural legacy of colonialism and imperialism. They had failed to deal with legacy issues in the former colonies where people of colour were called 'lazy natives' and treated with contempt or pity. He said that we in the west still regarded the Middle East and all lands east of Suez as inferior, backward, irrational and wild. Consequently, many young people in particular had developed a 'post-colonial syndrome', which he defined as a compound identity based on social, cultural, historical and political elements. In order to eradicate terrorism, one had first to deal with its source, namely post-colonial legacies. He recommended an approach based on Jungian psychology. What follows is a summary of what he said on the subject.

In Jungian psychology the Shadow is a dark force that resides within us and challenges the whole ego. It is the collective unconscious within human beings and it is not always confronted and raised to consciousness in the language of the human mind. It consists of repressed feelings, instincts and shortcomings that fester and blacken one's personality. Jung refers to it as the 'wolf soul'; in Chinese culture, however, it is more aptly described as the 'dragon soul'. The dragon is the dark shadow that resides within the Chinese mind. Unless individuals learn to control the Shadow within, they may project it onto others and there are no limits to its malign consequences. However, that is not the whole story. Jung also said that the Shadow is 90% pure gold. It can be our worst enemy or our best friend. It contains the primal drives of stone-age days. By engaging with the Shadow, we can release and sublimate our rejected selves. Jung added that when we walk the path of enlightenment, we find a foundation for our lives; we become rooted in a larger life that gives us resilience, endurance and meaning in a world that offers none of these things. In Chinese culture, the Shadow is identified as the Dragon, which is the embodiment of an ancient innate instinct. It tends to be at its darkest over legacy issues, especially misrule, racial discrimination, persecution and ethnic cleansing. Such abuses if allowed to fester, can distort one's moral judgement and engender a compulsive desire for retribution. Jung stated that there can be no light without the dark. We all have to learn how to control our emotions and discipline our minds. We have to remember to turn on the light even in the darkest of times. Unfortunately, oppressive regimes, past and present, do not seem to grasp the simple fact that one day, among the many people they have abused or victimised, there will be one who rises against them and strikes back.

When he said those things, I instantly began to see how aptly they fitted my experience of 'the dragon' that I had been chasing – the young lady we now knew as Estelle. One had to ask whether she was really a terrorist or a normal person concerned with the proper exercise of power and related moral questions. The people of Southeast Asia had been subject to massive misrule for over a century, most of it having its origin in colonialism since the time that Stamford Raffles had established a trading post in Singapore in 1819. The Chinese in particular had been abused and victimised not only by the colonial rulers but by their post-colonial national governments. It was hardly surprising therefore that some of them became radicalised. The big question for society is whether it is possible to de-radicalise such persons. The solution proposed by Professor Hammond was a greater focus on the cultivation of emotional intelligence. Obviously, every country had its own counter-terrorism measures and they worked to some extent but they did not deal with the problem of eradication.

Professor Hammond found that all the subjects in his case studies demonstrated high levels of intelligence but very low level of emotional intelligence which he defined as the ability to make emotions work for you. Emotional intelligence has many strands, the main ones being a high level of empathy, self-awareness, self-regulation and social skills. We are all the product of history and bear the scars of social and political inequality, coercion and manipulation. Emotional intelligence is not about being nice or gregarious; it is about managing our emotions in order to achieve the best possible outcomes. We all have to learn to how to form a connection with people at an emotional level. We all have to learn how to make emotions work for us instead of against us. We all have to learn how to use emotions to enhance thought and thus make better decisions. Those who let themselves be overwhelmed by their emotions dwell in darkness and, in Jungian terms, allow the Shadow to rule their lives.

In my line of work, we are told to 'know your enemy'. Our mentors in MI6 often tell us: 'Do not underestimate the intelligence of the malign creatures you seek to track down and apprehend. They are truly subhuman but they will have a high IQ.' It was clear to me that 'the dragon' I had been chasing was highly intelligent. She had eluded detection for the best part of a year in spite of robust surveillance by the security forces in Southeast Asia. Clearly, I was poorly equipped to understand her motivation. I wondered how she would react to a long custodial sentence in a British prison. Very few people in Britain were familiar with the work of Jung on the condition he called 'The Shadow', or the critical studies on post-colonialism by Edward Said. For most people, terrorists were 'the enemy within'. The prevailing UK mood on the issue of terrorism was summed up in the phrase 'lock them up and throw away the key. Terrorists are vermin and vermin must be exterminated.' Those on the right wing of the political spectrum argued that capital punished should be restored for acts of terrorism. Jihadists and terrorists were not just criminals; they were traitor and should be tried for treason and hanged in public. Foreign terrorists should be deported to their homeland. Very few people saw the problem as one of post-colonial alienation.

However, those who had experienced colonialism saw things differently. They saw the British establishment as the real villain. They distrusted a government with a long history of colonial exploitation and misrule and one which still supplied weapons of mass destruction to rogue states such as Saudi Arabia, the Gulf States, Israel and Malaysia. The British government hated people of colour, Muslims, Chinese, Arabs and anybody with a foreign face. It was hardly surprising that the victims of colonialism would strike back at their western oppressors as Che Guevara had done across Latin America and as Chin Peng had done in Malaya during the Emergency years. The oppressed would rise up and say to the oppressor: 'If you do not respect our life, our values, our culture and our people, we will make your life a living hell.'

Meanwhile Estelle had been placed under house arrest in the female wing of Loftus House in Victoria Street. It is a spartan detention centre known as 'Purgatory' where inmates suffer for a time before having their fate determined in court. There you are treated like a subhuman and named by a number. Estelle was 76. You get cold porridge for breakfast, a horrid salad for lunch and a foul-smelling stew for dinner. You spend a lot of time sitting on a wooden chair, gazing into space or perhaps reading a dog-eared and soiled novel. Estelle passed the time reading Roddy Doyle's 'The Woman Who Walked Into Doors.' She felt that she too had been there; she had walked into too many doors. She also did her yoga routines and practiced speaking aloud the speech she would deliver in court. 'My lord, may I explain how I came to this sad situation and with your permission may I spell out all tragic punishments that I as Chinese person suffered in my home country.' She had to choose her words carefully in a non-jury Special Criminal Court. She simply had to win the judge's better side. She had to convince him or her that her basic human rights had been trampled on. She had to make it clear that no British subject would tolerate such injustice, such blatant racism and such humiliation. However, she would remain cool, avoid any hint of hostility, show remorse for her misdeeds and appeal to the notion of British justice. She wrote down her strategy on the four pages of notepaper provided. She kept revising her text, speaking it aloud, paying attention to every word and getting the intonation right. She knew that she was good with words.

When Estelle looked in the mirror, she saw a fuzzy reflection staring back at her. She seemed to see aspects of her own totality – mind, heart, self, soul, feelings, flashing before her and she could sense a strange voice deep within her, exerting control over her. She kept asking herself: 'Who the hell am I? I am a mystery to myself. Am I really a normal person? What is normal?' Clearly, sooner or later she would have to unlock the door and seek answers from a 'knowing one' – from the Buddha or perhaps from an experienced psychiatrist. However, she was unlikely to get that opportunity before her trial.

THE TRIAL

It was in a climate of great national concern over terrorism that Estelle Fu-Cheng finally appeared before Justice Harvey in the Westminster Magistrates' Court on 15 December, 2003. It was not a good time to be charged with acts of terrorism. Fortunately for Estelle, Harvey was a liberal judge who did not believe in long prison sentences. Before the hearing, he had read and re-read the charge sheet, the book of evidence including the depositions of witnesses as well as my reports to MI6.

In British law, when a suspect pleads guilty to premeditated murder, no witnesses are called, no evidence is tested and the judge is required to hand down a mandatory 40-year sentence. If the suspects pleads guilty to conspiring to commit murder, a lesser sentence is handed down, usually a twenty-year prison sentence, with the possibility of early release for remorse and good conduct. Moreover, in law there are always extenuating circumstances which allow a judge to exercise a degree of autonomy. For instance, in the case of a confession, the problem for the judge is determining the truth value of the suspect's statements. In classical logic, a confession has only two values, true or false. Truth is a very elusive notion; one person's truth is another person's falsity. The line between the two is far from clear. Moreover, Judge Harvey was familiar with the much-publicised cases of suspects charged with subversion or sedition before the so-called Special Criminal Courts in Malaysia and Singapore. In Malaysia, suspects were routinely sent to a Detention Centre under the Sedition Act (1948) or the draconian Internal Security Act (ISA, 1960). While such abuses of basic human rights were regrettable, they did not in any way justify a person or group taking the law into their own hands. The right to life is the most fundamental of all human rights and the intentional taking of life can never be condoned. However, politically-motivated murder is a special case since in common law, one is permitted to defend one's territory, one's identity, one's human rights and one's very existence. At the trial, Judge Harvey had to satisfy himself on two crucial issues. Firstly, he had to be satisfied that the complex chain of events from its genesis in a remote Sarawakian town to its conclusion in a British Crown Court was legally sound and that there were no gaps in the evidence presented. Any alleged crimes committed by the suspect outside the UK were irrelevant to the case before him. He would strike out all the irrelevant evidence in the charge sheet. Stripped of its background, the present case was about a foreign national conspiring to do harm to another foreign national on British soil.

Secondly, he had to establish whether the case before him came under the heading of a terrorism offence, whether it was a personal vendetta or whether the suspect was of sound mind. He had reservations about the designation of the case as 'CPS terrorism'. It was true that it had been built jointly by MI5 and MI6 but the suspect was acting alone and not as a member of a terrorist group. An incorrect categorization of an alleged crime was very prejudicial. If a charge is wrongly worded, the presumption of innocence is reversed. Her profile seemed to indicate that she had been motivated by 'legacy issues' rather than malice. However, her confession speaks of 'voices in the head' and therefore I am forced to conclude that she is not of sound mind. She is unwell and needs therapy.

For Estelle, her day in court was not as disastrous as she had anticipated. The outcome was predetermined by her confession. She had wisely pleaded guilty to the charge of conspiring to kill the Commander of the Malaysian Special Branch, Abdul Razak bin Sharif and would have done so but for the intervention of MI6 and the MET. She accepted that she knowingly intended to commit a criminal act and she acknowledged her guilt on that count, while at the same time claiming that her action was morally justifiable since each of her victims richly deserved to be punished for their criminal actions and abuse of power. Does not the Bible ordain that the just man scatter the evil one like chaff? Estelle still recalled one of the biblical citations frequently quoted by the Principal at St. Mary's Mission School: 'I will scatter them like chaff driven by the desert wind.' (Jeremiah 13:24). However, Judge Harvey, dismissed her argument saying: 'In my court I dispense civil law, not the law of God. It is best that we allow the Almighty to deal with the ungodly.'

The trial was something of a non-event. Since Estelle had already confessed to conspiring to commit a felony in London, there was no need to sift through the evidence or call witnesses. In Judge Harvey's mind, the defendant was not a 'terrorist' as defined in British law. She was an outcast in her homeland, a second-class citizen, a defender of the rights of an oppressed race, beginning with the misrule by the former colonial rulers of British Malaya and British Borneo and continuing with the same race-based policies by the Federal government in Putrajaya. According to her police profile, she was a dangerous serial killer. She had 'executed' (her word) seven British subjects already and was planning to 'terminate' (her word) the chief of the Malaysian Special Branch. Since Judge Harvey ruled that her previous actions in Southeast Asia, however unlawful, were irrelevant to the trial, he dismissed the 'terrorism' plea of the Crown Prosecution Service (CPS). Moreover, he was of the opinion that Estelle was carrying a lot of emotional trauma which was inconsistent with the charge of being named a pathological 'serial killer'. The problem for Harvey was how to reconcile the demands of British law with the rights of a young Chinese woman to defend a number of basic human rights, which in his summary, he listed as follows:

1) All persons born and raised in a country are entitled to full citizenship of that country and all the benefits that full citizenship entails. No person is a second class citizen or a non-citizen.

2) All citizens, irrespective of race, religion, or sexual orientation are entitled to be treated with dignity and respect. Legal equality and equality of opportunity are the hallmarks of a civilised society.

3) In a multiracial society, each ethnic group is entitled to enjoy protection under the law on the basis of both legal-constitutional and historical-cultural factors.

4) All citizens are entitled to freedom of speech, freedom of assembly and freedom of religion in a plural society.

During the trial Estelle remained calm and said very little other than to insist that violence begets violence and that her intended targets 'deserved to die'. Naturally, the judge did not agree. He stated that murder was a heinous crime. There was one fundamental human right that was the entitlement of every human being, and that right was the right of life. No person or government had the right to extinguish the right to life of another human being. If that right is removed, society lapses into barbarism.

Accordingly, he was obliged to find Estelle guilty of the grave felony of planning the unlawful killing of another person. The fact that she had not actually carried out her plan was irrelevant. Mens rea was clearly present. He had no compunction, therefore, in handing down a twenty-year prison sentence in a high-security British prison for females. However, on the balance of probability, he concluded that Estelle was not of sound mind. Her confession referred to 'voices in the head' and her psychological report also indicated that she seemed to present symptoms of psychosomatic stress or possibly early-stage schizophrenia. Like the doctor in Macbeth (Act 5) he concluded that 'more needs she the divine than the physician'. Moreover, in view of her remorse and compunction for her misdeeds and the possibility that she was not of sound mind, he was willing to allow Estelle to serve a shorter custodial sentence in a Category C prison under certain conditions. In Britain, even prisons have a class system denoted as Category A, B, C and D. Category C prisons are for offenders labelled 'extremists' due to mental health problems. Based on her psychological assessment, Judge Harvey concluded that Estelle needed therapy rather than a penal sentence. He saw no reason why she should not be returned to the healing and supportive environment of Chatsworth Manor where under the wise mentorship of Lady Sophy and Dr. Dell she would dispel the darkness in her soul. He therefore deemed it proper to suspend the twenty-year sentence if she undertook to participate in a rehabilitation program conducted by Dr. Dell and his team at Chatsworth. She would serve time in that modern 'Correctional Institution' for a period not exceeding two-and-a-half years. She would undergo a programme of behavioural correction, after which, if successful, her case would be reviewed and she could be granted early release. However, if she failed to respond to the corrective therapy, she would be transferred to HM Prison at Downview where she would spend the remainder of her twenty-year custodial sentence.

Before closing the trial, Judge Harvey said to Estelle: 'I know you want a just society, as we all do, but you must not engage in violence in order to bring it about. You cannot go back and change the past, but you can start where you are and change the future'.

Not everyone was pleased with the unexpected outcome of the trial. The British media berated Judge Harvey for not making the punishment fit the crime. The right-wing press in particular scoffed at the notion of pampering dangerous criminals like Estelle Fu-Cheng in a posh 'holiday home' run by the 'The Glebe Foundation' and paid for by British taxpayers. 'Send her back where she belongs,' the headlines screamed 'We will not pay for her rehabilitation.' On leaving the court, Judge Harvey was accosted by a smart-ass reporter from the 'Daily Dispatch' who said: 'You have said that the accused demonstrated real compunction. Now, that's a funny word. How do you define 'compunction?' Quick as a flash, Harvey replied: 'I always act in good conscience. As for 'compunction' I should rather feel it than know its definition. Good day!'

Bonner-Davies and I saw the judgement as fair and humane. Clearly, Estelle's case was more about the actions of a misguided civil rights activist rather than a Chinese villain seeking revenge. The verdict was based on the belief that nobody is beyond redemption. One had to deal with the problem of radicalisation in a more enlightened way than dumping the offender in prison, where he or she remained obdurate in their evil ideology and even radicalised other prisoners. Category C prisons offered offenders a new beginning, so to speak, in coming to terms with the problem of terrorism and radicalisation, which Judge Harvey predicted would become the greatest menace facing Britain in the coming years. As for Estelle, she felt like giving the judge a big Chinese hug, but of course, that was out of the question. She might, however, send him a red rose one day. She wanted him to know that she was ready and willing to get back on the road to enlightenment.

CHATSWORTH MANOR

'The Chatsworth Foundation' is a modern version of the old British institution known as a 'House of Correction'. In former times, Chatsworth Manor had been the country residence of the owners of the Vanderbilt Merchant Bank, which collapsed during the financial crisis of 1990–91. It is a splendid neo-classical building, designed by the great Victorian architect Thomas Morrison for the wealthy Chatsworth family in the 1880s. It is set in the beautiful rolling Surrey countryside, near the village of Egham. Originally, it stood on an estate of over 500 acres of pasture land, liberally planted with giant redwoods and beech trees. When it was purchased by the Vanderbilts, most of the wooded estate was sold off and the manor house was extended at the rear. With the collapse of the bank and the recession that followed in the early 90s, Chatsworth Manor was taken over by the Heritage Society and subsequently leased to the government as a rehabilitation centre for female prisoners. It is ironic that such an imposing residence should end up as the home of hardened criminals whose crimes shocked the nation. It some respects, Chatsworth Manor is similar many of the stately mansions that dot the English countryside except that its accommodation is more austere and the food is not quite gourmet. You would never guess that the happy smiling residents detained there were incarcerated women, doing time for violent crimes. In effect, they were internees and were not allowed to go beyond the imposing wrought iron entry gates to the estate. The officer at the front desk could observe every move as inmates passed through security scanners on their way to and from the playing areas, the swimming poor and the Arts and Craft Centre which was housed in what used to be the old stables and outhouses.

The philosophy of the Chatsworth Foundation is one of redemption and rehabilitation rather than punishment and incarceration. The objective is to deradicalise the inmates by a well-planned program of remedial therapy based on Jungian psychology. The inmates are not on medication of any kind. Any inmate found to be disruptive or violet is discharged to the prison system. Visiting by family members is allowed at weekends. There is a chapel for Christians and a prayer room for Muslims. Inmates are confined to their cells from 10 p.m. Windows are not barred as in a prison but doors are locked at night.

On arrival at Chatsworth Manor, Estelle was greeted by the charming manager, Lady Sophy Cunningham, who said: 'Welcome to our humble abode. It's not exactly the Hilton, but there are worse places for young ladies needing rest and rehabilitation.' Lady Sophy was a devout Methodist and she ran Chatsworth Manor much like a Methodist boarding school, meaning, no smoking, no drugs, no alcohol, no sex, no bad language, no disruptive behaviour and no quarrelling with inmates. At Chatsworth, the words 'prison, governor, warden and prison officer' do not apply. All staff members are 'Correctional Officers' and the manager is not called the Governor; she is called the Head. Some of the inmates call her 'the Mother Superior' and all address her as Lady Sophy.

Estelle found her new home congenial, warm and welcoming. Like the other inmates, she had several places to go: the common room, the library, the sports centre, the cafeteria, the work station, the chapel or her cell. It was her choice as to where and how she she passed her free time. As in the army, there was a wake-up call at 7.30 a.m. followed by breakfast at 8 a.m. From 9 to 10 a.m. everyone was required to undertake some form of manual labour. The home, like a monastery, is largely self-sufficient, with its own vegetable garden, an enclosure for goats and hens, a bakery for bread making, a dairy etc. There was also a good-sized vegetable garden. There, under the watchful eye of the aging Mr. Roberts, the head gardener, inmates learned how to grow food sustainably without pesticides or artificial fertilizers and how to use leaf-mould to feed next year's plants. Residents were free to choose the kind of activity that they felt most suited for. They were also allowed to attend one or more of the many training or educational courses on offer, such as business study, IT applications, nature study, Bible study, etc. All inmates were required to attend one counselling session with Dr. Dell each week, as well as one group counselling session. An inmate might, if she wished, request additional private time with Dr. Dell.

The most popular place at Chatsworth is the Arts and Craft Centre which gives the inmates a wonderful avenue of creativity. It extends over the old stables and outhouses, with a variety of work areas, benches, tools, machines and storage containers for materials. It was Lady Sophy's idea. She knew that her girls needed to gain access to art, working with textiles, ceramics, basket weaving, wood carving, costume jewelry and other useful handicrafts. Many of the handicrafts obviously had potential commercial values, especially art, pottery, wickerwork, garment repair, dog grooming, etc. There was also a section dedicated to specific life skills, such as cookery, dress making, garment repairs, leather work, rag toys, music making etc. Living in the digital age, one had of necessity to become IT savvy and of course everyone had a state-of-the-art smartphone not only for chatting on social media but also for access to 'how to do it' menus on the Internet. The satisfaction that one gets from making something, be it a simple task like jam making, or painting a garden fence, is enormous and at Chatsworth it had the added advantage of creating a bond of friendship and cooperation between the inmates, as they talked about and shared their work experience. Furthermore, on the first Saturday of each month, there was a Sale of Work, open to the public at which the inmates sold their produce and gained some extra income to supplement their Social Welfare allowance. Once a week, in groups of ten, they were allowed to visit the village of Chatsworth for shopping, banking and other personal services.

Estelle was new to working with her hands. In Malaysia, every family has an amah who does all the cooking and housework. When she left school, she did not know how to cook an egg or change a light bulb. Now, at last, she discovered how to do things with her own hands and it gave her enormous satisfaction. She decided to have a go at soap making, using the cold process. Herbalism was her secret passion and like all Chinese people she was fastidious about cleanliness and the use of organic ingredients. Ideally, should have liked to walk the hills and dales to find and collect yarrow, chamomile, lemon balm, gorse, lavender and peppermint. The only useful plants at her disposal on the farm were clover, nettles and wild roses. In that case, her best option was to purchase lye and essential oils online. Once you have the necessary basic equipment, all you need for soap making is water, lye and oil. Estelle's soap making venture created an enormous buzz among her comrades and they all wanted her handmade lemon soap.

Most of the inmates at Chatsworth Manor had no desire to be released into society. They were quite content to remain as guests of the nation, all paid for by the British taxpayer. They were given a free run of the building and the recreational areas at the rear. These included a hockey playing pitch, tennis courts and a cycle track around the High Field at the rear. The entire compound was cut off the outside world by ten-foot-high perimeter fence. Within the compound, inmates enjoyed freedom of movement. However, Lady Sophy insisted that one golden rule be observed at all times. That rule was one word, 'Respect'. All staff and inmates had to observe absolute respect for each other. She was especially solicitous for the welfare of inmates from overseas. She had in former times served as a prison officer in Hong Kong. She did not speak a word of Chinese but she held the Chinese in high esteem and she made sure that Chinese New Year was properly celebrated each year in her Correctional Centre. She always looked on the bright side of life and did her best to enrich the lives of the inmates. She believed that 'her girls', as she called them, would mellow in the caressing warmth of Chatsworth Manor. She had evocative paintings on the walls and magnificent Persian carpets on the floor of the living room and the library. She believed that beautiful things made beautiful people. Over the classic Victorian marble fireplace in the entrance hall, she had hung a museum reproduction of Claude Monet's great painting 'Femmes au Jardin.' showing elegant young ladies in gay dresses disporting themselves on the lawn under the green leafy shade of the trees, merging with the foliage and the shrubbery. It was, in Lady Sophy's opinion, an object lesson in good deportment, good manners and good feminine behaviour.

Lady Sophy is very proud of the fact that almost all of her girls go on to rediscover their dignity and put their bad ways behind them. On release, they go back into the world with life skills, good manners and self-confidence. Not one of her girls has ever re-offended. She explains her success by saying that 'a spoonful of honey will catch more flies than a bottle of vinegar.' She says almost all of the inmates have hearts of gold but have been badly abused by society. She knows how women overseas are often denied their basic human rights unless they join and support the ruling establishment. However, she does not approve of terrorist tactics and killing. She tells Estelle that all life is sacred and that human killing is never justified. However, Estelle has still to make up her mind on that issue. 'In the words of Fidel Castro', she says 'history will absolve me.'

LOOKING IN THE MIRROR

Estelle counts her blessings that her life at Chatsworth Manor is stress free and not at all punitive. Lady Sophy radiates charm and positivity. 'We are all on a journey', she tells the girls under her charge and she never refers to them as internees, which is what they really are. She quite likes the fact that she is known and the 'Mother Superior'. She would say that her place was more like a Benedictine Abbey than a Category C prison. There was ample time for reflection and soul searching.

Estelle spends a good deal of time gazing into space, trying to figure out who she is, freely roaming backward in her mind to her early years, her schooling in Kuching and her mingling with 'normal' people at the University of Australia in Canberra. She keeps asking herself why her life has become a long river of alienation, unease, tension and strife. It carries her along through raging torrents, dark pools and over rapids to an unknown destination. Right now, she hardly knows whether she is a normal person or a properly confused idealist. She wants to believe Lady Sophy who assures her that there is hope and light at the end of the tunnel. She wonders whether that is just a pious Methodist aspiration or if it might be true.

Looking back at her schooling at St. Mary's Mission School in Kuching, much had faded from her memory. What surprised her most was what the teachers there did NOT tell you. They were all devout Anglicans but chose not to voice any criticism of the government nor to mention the shocking episode of British colonialism across Southeast Asia. Her history teacher, Mr. Keith Robinson, even suggested that colonial rule had somehow prepared the natives for self-rule in the Malay states, Singapore and Burma. The history syllabus designed by the Islamic gurus in the Federal government erased many important episodes and personages. For instance, it did not mention the role of Kapitan Yap Ai Loy as the founder of Kuala Lumpur. It did not mention the exploitation of Indian workers on the rubber plantations in Malacca nor the abuse of Chinese workers in the tin mines in the Kinta Valley. It did not say much about the colonisation of Penang by Francis Light and the East India Company. It glossed over the colonisation of Sarawak by the White Rajahs and the acquisition of Sabah by the North Borneo Chartered Company. It ignored Chin Peng and his comrades who conducted the armed revolt known as 'the Emergency' (1948-1960). It called them brigands, communists and terrorists, whereas in fact they were freedom fighters. Their fight for national freedom had to be erased from the history books. The erasing of history is something the government was good at.

Estelle could not understand why Anglicans in Sarawak held the White Rajahs and other British colonists is high esteem. She recalled the devout Anglican convictions of the Principal, Miss Timms, who at assembly would point to the large Philips map of world showing the vast British Empire in pink and say: 'Children, we must never forget how fortunate we are that our state was born within the great British Empire which brought us good governance and civility.' Estelle remembers wincing at the words 'good governance' and 'civility. 'What a load of codswallop!' she would mutter to herself. She knew very well what the British had brought to Southeast Asia; they brought the Bible and took the land. In her mind, that was not a fair exchange. They spoke of the 'white man's burden' towards the coloured races – the 'lazy natives' who needed uplifting and protection. Every dog on the street knew very well that the British colonists brought race-based ideology, apartheid, unbounded greed and exploitation. However, she dare not speak her mind. In Malaysia you have to be careful what you say and do. The walls have ears and the streets have eyes. The Special Branch (SB) has moles everywhere and its Director of Operations is determined to crack down on subversives, socialists, bloggers, political activists and disgruntled Chinese and Indians. Any criticism of the government could land you in trouble. You could be branded 'enemies of the state' and detained under the notorious Internal Security Act (ISA). You could be arrested and detained without trial in the Taiping Detention Centre in Perak. You might even be disappeared. The Special Branch operated above the law. One of its aims was the suppression of Chinese culture and the elimination of all Chinese and Indian 'hot heads'. When it came to dirty tricks the Special Branch had few equals.

One of things that Estelle still finds most troubling is racism not only in Malaysia but in many countries worldwide, even in Britain. At school in Kuching, she learned about the shocking slave trade when black people were called 'niggers', were bought and sold, were abused, humiliated and treated as subhuman. She had read about the inhuman conditions which slaves endured on the cotton fields and sugar plantations. In law, they that had no more value than a piece of furniture. And even though slavery was abolished in Britain in 1833 and in the British Raj in 1860, it continued underground for over a hundred years. From her perspective, racism was deeply ingrained in the British psyche. She knew how waves of coloured immigrants to Britain from the former colonies in Africa, the Indian subcontinent and the Caribbean had been subjected to a torrent of racial abuse. Sometimes, the abuse was explicit as in the hate speech of MPs such as Enoch Powell whose 'Rivers of Blood' speech (1968) articulated the latent racial prejudice of many white British people to mass immigration from the Commonwealth. Of course, it was not only black people who were targeted. Racial abuse was also meted out to the Irish, the Germans and the French – all of whom were collectively branded 'bloody foreigners'. In London, Manchester and Liverpool many lodging houses posted a notice on the front door, saying: 'Sorry, no blacks or Irish.' In London, xenophobia was especially pronounced in Tory boroughs where one heard the comment 'The wogs begin at Calais.' Consequently, Estelle was not surprised that some of the worst racial prejudice was reserved for the Chinese, who were referred to as the 'Yellow Peril'. She also wondered why it was that practically all the detainees in Chatsworth were coloured people.

Estelle's abiding discontent was the race-based ideology of the ruling coalition in Malaysia and the fact that the country was becoming a police state. She referred to the BN coalition in the national parliament as the 'Malay Muslim Mafia'. Of course, the great majority of Malaysians, including many Chinese and Indians, were quite happy to have a strong Islamic government. They knew it was corrupt but they voted for it in order to get a slice of the salami. One could see that the winds of change were blowing across Europe. At least some people were standing up for equality, human rights and racial harmony but in Southeast Asia the status quo remained just as toxic and racist as in colonial times, based on the racist headline set by the colonial administration. Malaysia still adhered to the 'divide and rule' principle of its former masters. There was no respect for the traditional moral values of the Chinese race, or that of the Indian race or that of the indigenous people. Apart from Chin Peng in former times, nobody seemed willing to stand up against misrule and racist discrimination. Of course, Chin Peng was branded a traitor. His uprising failed because of lack of public support and he was forced to flee the country. He did not belong; consequently, he became a footnote in the history books – a maverick, a mad Chinese idealist, a leftist rebel backed by China.

Even though she was aggrieved at the 'old colonial' stance of the teachers, Estelle could not fault the quality of tuition at St. Mary's. It was one of the best schools in Sarawak. In 1988 she sat the Cambridge A-level Examination and scored straight As in Chinese, English and History. Her parents hoped that she would go on to study law at the University of Singapore but Estelle had other ideas. She decided to continue her studies at the Australian National University (ANU) in Canberra where she enrolled in the Southeast Asian Studies (SIAS) programme.

From day one, she loved Canberra, its multiracial people, its splendid architecture and most of all its wonderful university. On campus she felt free as a bird and she fervently hoped that her time there would help to heal her emotional scars. She was amazed at the depth and width of the SIAS course and profound knowledge of its director, Professor Freeman, a man of liberal views and enormous scholarship. He is an expert on the history of Southeast Asia and having lectured in colleges there from Burma to Borneo, he knows about the political background of the Malay states going back to the Majapahit Kingdom which spread across the region from Java long before the Muslim conquest and colonial expansion by the British, Dutch and Spanish. It was the first time that Estelle heard about the Majapahit period which is never mentioned in school textbooks in Malaysia. What she found most revealing was Professor Freeman's discourse on the concept of kingship and his claim that the race-based politics of modern Malaysia could be traced back to the elite values and norms of the Majapahit feudal politics, long before racial ideology became the cornerstone of British colonialism. Furthermore, he described the ruling party, BN, as a neo-feudal elite-led coalition requiring blind obedience to the leader and it followed that the nation's administration and coffers must be forever in the safe hands of the Malay Muslim majority. What was even more remarkable was his contention that the Malaysian school curriculum and teachers' beliefs and attitudes established norms and behavioural control over students. The hidden curriculum was an instrument of indoctrination. He also stated that real democracy did not exist anywhere in Southeast Asia, even in Singapore. In his view, each member state of ASEAN was modelled on the old feudal system, with the ruler and his elite at her top of the pyramid and the landless peasants at the bottom. He said that Malaysia, Brunei, Borneo and Burma were 'to a greater of lesser extent monarchical kingdoms, mere sham democracies, where the power and wealth rested in the hands of the elite.' At times, Professor Freeman seemed to be articulating Estelle's thesis that Malaysia was no place for people of Chinese, Indian or Indonesian origin. Even intellectual Malay Muslims agreed that the government was rotten to the core. The big unanswered question was how to change an entrenched corrupt system.

At tutorials and seminars Estelle stood out especially whenever Professor Freeman was present. She knew that he was just as passionate about human rights and civil liberties as she was. On one occasion when the topic under discussion was how to react to state-sponsored discrimination, she caused quite a stir when asked what she might do about it in Sarawak. Her reply was: 'Well, I may have to sling a few bombs around!' Prophetic words!

On her return to Kuching in 2002, all of her happy memories of life in Canberra and the four years spent at ANU came gushing back to her mind. She could see that nothing had changed in her absence. In fact, things had got much worse as more scandals were uncovered in government circles. She soon discovered that there are none so deaf as those who do not want to hear. She knew that evil had to be confronted and that she would have to stand up and fight especially when nobody else seemed to care. She made her plan and prepared herself for her mission. Everything had gone according to plan except for her final operation in London where she had made a fatal blunder. She should have known better. She has acted rashly. The Great Master, Sun Tzu, would not have approved. He would have waited a few days for the dust to settle. He would not have walked into the trap set by MI6. Now, all she can say is 'mea culpa!' And now, as she lay on her bed in Chatsworth Manor, she wondered whether her whole operation had been worthwhile. She wondered why she, just like Chin Peng, was obsessed with defending democracy. Perhaps her approach was too extreme. Perhaps she should have listened to Professor Freeman who once said: 'The worst form of democracy is better than killing.'

However, things could have been much worse. She could have been sent to a high-security prison for 20 years. However, she was fortunate that her case had been heard by the liberal Judge Harvey who took the view that we all make mistakes and deserve the chance to redeem ourselves. In Estelle's eyes, he was a wise man, just like Professor Freeman. Then, on her return to Chatsworth Manor, Lady Sophy had assured her that Dr. Dell would to help her on the road to recovery. She told Estelle that he was a gentleman and a scholar, a man who had read Noam Chomsky on the death of democracy and Edward Said on postcolonial ideology. He would be aware of the alienation engendered by a Malay-centric government with a narrow tunnel vision. Furthermore, he had immersed himself deeply in Jungian psychology. She was confident that he would help Estelle come to terms with her legacy issues. She said: 'We are all shaped and often wounded by external factors but we need to look within ourselves as well.' She also added two further comments which Estelle took to heart. She said, 'I understand where you are coming from and I know that your future lies in the past. That is true for all of us. But I also know that there is a fine line between good and evil. That line must not be crossed. You need help.'

In response Estelle said the word 'understood'. She knew that Lady Sophy was reading her mind and she decided it was time to open the door to her inner self. She needed therapy and peace of mind.

REFORMING THE DRAGON

Estelle took to her therapy like a duck to water. She found great satisfaction in the confessional narrative of her life, her fears, her alienation and her confidence to put things right. She liked Dr. Dell. He was a gentleman of the old school, a tall figure with compassionate eyes and an infectious smile. There was a silent strength to him – a rootedness that one usually finds in gardeners, grandparents and old soldiers. Dr. Dell was not anchored to his desk but preferred to walk with his client down the sweeping driveway leading to Chatsworth Manor, past box-hedged lawns, giving way to a large paddock with giant redwoods and beech trees. On reaching the front gate, the pair would take the narrow pathway round the high field to the rear of the manor house and pause for a while in the bower by the perimeter wall at the northern end of the walkway. There, they would be enraptured by birdsong and the balm of wild flowers in what Estelle described as 'a sauna of sensual delight.'

Dr. Dell is a Jungian psychologist and as such he holds that one's personality is shaped by the 'Shadow', which is the suppressed part of our psyche, in other words, the unconscious self which the conscious ego does not identify. Jung held that we are all caught between the voice of the conscious mind and the voice of our collective unconscious mind, i.e., our innate psyche, which may be deep and dark or brimful of light and wisdom. The 'Shadow' can be our worst enemy or our best friend. It can be our dark side, or our seat of creativity. It contains the primal drives of stone-age days. By engaging with the 'Shadow', we can release and sublimate our long-lost rejected selves. Jung said that when we walk the path of enlightenment, we find a foundation for our lives; we become rooted in a larger life that gives us resilience, endurance, and meaning in a world that offers none of these things. Dr. Dell went further and held that the 'Shadow' is a culturally transmitted phenomenon which resides in oral tradition, storytelling, poetry, art, music and the lore of a particular tribe. He did not have to spell out the fact that in Chinese culture, the 'Dragon' is the 'Shadow'. Estelle had already made the connection and it all made sense to her.

Dr. Dell went on to explain that whether we call it the 'Shadow' or the 'Dragon', it is an ancient innate instinct for survival, which we all need, but if not properly controlled, it can distort one's moral and mental judgement. Turning to the situation in her homeland, he agreed that the world needs revolutionaries and reformers but at the same time one has to recognize, manage and regulate emotions in oneself and in others in order to achieve goals. The 'Dragon' was pure gold if it enabled you to use emotions to enhance thought and make better decisions.

It seems that Estelle took Dr. Dell's words to heart and she spent many hours in quiet reflection seeking practical ways and means to regulate her raw emotions. She would have to re-set her emotional control device so as to tune in to the good voice of the 'Dragon'. She would have to take positive steps to overcome her alienation and her disaffection with the situation in her homeland. In positive thinking, prompted by the 'Dragon', every problem has a solution that need not entail violence. Obviously, killing people was too crude an instrument to redress past wrongs. There had to be a better way and over the coming weeks and months Dr. Dell would teach her how to cope with and resolve the many social and human rights issues that she faced in her homeland. He would be her mentor. She would learn to be at peace within herself and discover how to start the long process of social and political reform in society.

19

ONCE A DRAGON...

As the weeks passed, Estelle got to know several of the Chatsworth inmates quite well. Their crimes exceeded hers by a mile in both gravity and gruesomeness. For instance, Ayesha, an attractive Pakistani girl in her 20s told her how her landlord in Bradford tried to rape her and how she cut his throat from ear to ear with a flick knife. For good measure, she also severed his penis. She could not afford a defence lawyer and she was given a life sentence, which was later found to be unsafe and she ended up in Chatsworth Manor.

Another British-African inmate, Nafisa, whose family came from Sudan, was arrested outside the Sudanese Embassy in London and charged with causing grievous bodily harm to the First Secretary when he attempted to address the chanting protestors who accused the Sudanese government of genocide in Southern Sudan. She knocked him unconscious with her knobkerrie, for which she was given five years behind bars. However, her sentence was appealed and having served two years in prison, she was sent to Chatsworth Manor.

A Libyan student nurse, Selma Bashiri, described how she went to her local butcher's shop in Croydon to buy halal meat. The cheeky butcher said: 'We do not sell that rubbish here.' She took that to be an insult against Islam and grabbing a cleaver she chopped off his right hand which he had raised to protect his face. For her crime, she was sentenced to five years behind bars. She served one year at Brixton Prison and was then transferred to Chatsworth Manor.

Several of the inmates were serving time for terrorism-related offences. They remained aloof and did not speak about their organisation or their crime. The exception was Mandy, a femme fatale from London, who had amassed considerable wealth by spying for a foreign power. She was the mistress of a senior officer in the Ministry of Defence from whom, in return for sex, she had obtained classified information. She was known to the inmates as 'Randy Mandy'. She was always full of jollity and tall tales. She was planning to retire to the south of France when her sentence expired in 2010.

In 2004, Chinese New Year fell on 22nd January, a cold bleak day in mid-winter. The event was duly celebrated in Chatsworth Manor. Mandy had arranged for a splendid Dragon dance. She had hired a band of six shaven-headed Chinese boys to perform the dragon dance. The dance then merged into a fancy dress party and ended with a fireworks display on the front lawn. Everyone had a fun time as they welcomed the Year of the Monkey.

Because of the celebrations, the inmates were allowed an extra hour's grace before retiring for the night at 11 p.m. Outside the manor house, a fierce storm was raging through the giant redwoods and beech trees. Gale force winds lashed the south facade of Chatsworth Manor. On such a night, it was good to have the warmth and comfort of a cozy cell in a stately building. All over the area, the storm was causing devastation. However, one inmate braved the elements on that stormy night. That person was Estelle. The storm was a major crisis for London and the Home counties but for Estelle it was an unexpected opportunity to carry out her daring plan. She had already made links with the underground pro-democracy Chinese students in London. Together, they had hatched the great escape. It was planned to coincide with Chinese New Year celebrations. Estelle viewed the chaotic storm damage with relief. Serendipity was writ large on her face as she recalled the words of the great master, Sun Tzu: 'Never waste a good crisis.' She climbed out of the window of her cell on the first floor, shinned down a pillar, dashed across the windswept courtyard to the sheds at the rear of the building. Then, hidden from view, she climbed over the boundary wall with the aid of a rope which suddenly appeared, thrown by an unseen hand. Within minutes, she was riding pillion on a motorcycle heading to Heathrow Airport.

That stormy night in London and Surrey is known as 'the night of the mighty wind'. Gale force winds blew the roofing off many old Victorian houses, uprooted trees and brought down power lines. It was followed by a massive downpour and extensive flooding. In the ensuing chaos, nobody had noticed that Estelle had made good her escape. It was 7 a.m. that morning before the Met were alerted to the fact. Naturally, Det. Superintendent Flanagan and his team swung into action, sealing off all exit points from Chatsworth and the surround area. Soon the whole area around Staines and Egham was swarming with Special Branch officer on motorcycles, squad cars and helicopters. Foot patrols began combing the woods and field around Chatsworth with sniffer dogs but all in vain. The bird had flown.

On arrival at Heathrow, Estelle was given a change of clothing, an Indonesian passport, a large cache of US dollars and a one-way air ticket to Dubai. She waved goodbye to London and to her friends in Chatsworth Manor. Nobody knows what happened to her subsequently. To this day, her whereabouts is a mystery. We know that from Dubai, she sent a red rose to Justice Harvey at the Special Criminal Court and on the attached greeting card were the cryptic words: 'Kind regards from the wayward one. Moving on. Estelle.'

Shortly after 9 a.m. Flanagan managed to make contact with MI5 and MI6. At that time Bonner-Davies was in Malta, where he was having urgent talks with our agent over the worsening situation in Libya. Flanagan began: 'You may have heard that we had a mighty storm here last night and guess what. The Dragon has done a runner. I repeat, Ms. Fu-Chin has leaped over the wall and has disappeared without a trace.'

Bonner-Davies replied: 'Well, my good friend. That's hardly surprising. After all, once a dragon, always a dragon! According to David Attenborough, they don't like confined spaces.'

Flanagan, however, was in no mood for banter, saying: 'Old Naylor in MI5 will have a fit. Please tell him that it's not over yet; that we are hot on her heels, which of course is a damned lie. She has probably made it to Heathrow and may well be on her way to God-knows-where. We cannot even contact Departures at Heathrow. All the lines are down. We're really in the soup right now.'

I felt sorry for Flanagan. I was back in Kuching at that time and it was several hours later that Bonner-Davies contacted me and instructed me to proceed forthwith to KL International Airport in case Estelle turned up. He had arranged for the head of the Special Branch, Abdul Razak, to meet me there so as to 'greet' Estelle on her arrival. Of course, we knew instinctively that she would not show. She had probably skedaddled to Amsterdam or Dublin or Paris, gone through Immigration on a fake passport and was already planning her next hop.

Nobody has ever discovered the identity of the motorcycle driver nor the identity of the person who planned the escape. Of course, fingers were pointed at Mandy, who was well known to the Chinese community in Staines. However, she denied any involvement in the affair. Clearly, she had the contacts and the cash to mastermind such a daring undertaking. When Lady Sophy asked her if she was involved in Estelle's escape, she replied: 'Of course not. Would I ever do such a thing?' Of course, everyone knew she would.

MI6 believes that Estelle was granted political asylum on a remote Indonesian island, of which there are 17,500. However, my impression is that neither Bonner Davies, nor Flanagan wish to know where she is. One thing that we all agree on is that she no longer wished to live in a corrupt theocratic state. As for me, I hope she is in a better place, not only geographically but within herself. She has not returned to Sarawak and her family in Kuching say they have no idea where she is; of course, they would say that, wouldn't they? According to our man in Makassar, she is now living in some style on a remote island beyond Lombok. There, on that exotic and peaceful island, among the gentle Sasak people, she probably hopes to rebuild her shattered life and find peace and enlightenment. That remote island is home to the Komodo dragon – a very dangerous animal. Local people will tell you that there is now one more dragon on the island!

--THE END--

Printed in the United States
by Baker & Taylor Publisher Services